Adam Brown Todd

The Circling Year, and Other Poems

Adam Brown Todd

The Circling Year, and Other Poems

ISBN/EAN: 9783744712002

Printed in Europe, USA, Canada, Australia, Japan

Cover: Foto ©Andreas Hilbeck / pixelio.de

More available books at **www.hansebooks.com**

CONTENTS.

———o———

1

JOHN FRANCIS WALLER, Esq., LL.D.,

VICE-PRESIDENT OF THE ROYAL DUBLIN SOCIETY,

&c. &c. &c.

———o———

DEAR SIR,

I dedicate " The Circling Year " to you, not so much because of the high and well-deserved place which you have long occupied in the walks of literature, as because no living poet, for the last quarter of a century, has been so often in my thoughts as yourself ; and also because that, ever since I made your acquaintance as a writer, no one has afforded me a purer or a more exquisite pleasure. I have returned again and again, with ever-increasing delight, to your incomparable " Slingsby Papers ; " and very often, as I have rambled among the green hills of Scotia in the balmy, dreamy summer days, or traversed her purple moors in the mellow autumn time, I have breathed aloud your beautiful, and to me matchless, lyrics, upon the light winds which wantoned among the green glens, and along the banks of many a lonely, limpid, tinkling stream which gush and meander around the sources of the Ayr, the Lugar, the Afton, and the Nith ; upon or near to the beautiful banks and braes of which I have passed the greater part of my life.

Thus, though I have never seen you in the body, and it is but recently that I have been honoured by your correspondence and friendship, and by your approving encouragement; yet I have long been intimate with you in spirit, and so feel, even now, as if I was addressing myself to one with whom I had long been personally familiar.

In the following Poems I have not designedly imitated any school of poetry or any author, so far as I know, unless it be in the mere structure of the verse.

Born in the country, and reared to agricultural and pastoral pursuits, amid scenes of picturesque beauty, and of stirring and often hallowed historical associations; and trained by a noble, pious, and poetic mother, my heart was early captivated by the loveliness and the sublimities of Nature, and moved and fired in no ordinary degree by gazing upon the battle scenes of bygone ages, where our forefathers bravely fought for their civil liberty, and for their religious faith; and where, in the stirring Covenanting times, they often conquered even when they fell. My mind has become attached to such scenes, and especially to the quiet retirement of the country, in an almost overmastering degree; and my happiest hours have been spent alone, or with some loved companion of congenial tastes, in traversing the trackless wilds, threading the pathless woods, tracing the unpolluted streams which run among the hills, or in gazing upon the rippling waters of some lonesome loch far in among the mountains, and watching the little waves chasing each other on to the green or silvery shore.

To me, the grandest picture-gallery has always been the ever-changing clouds of heaven, and especially those around the morning chambers of the sun; and in among the great glowing curtains which he gathers around his burning brow, as he rolls down the western sky on a calm summer night, and sinks from sight behind the splintered pinnacles of the hills in Arran's isle, all flickering and glowing in rays of rosy, saffron, or orange light; while down below, and far around, the wide waters of the Frith of Clyde glow like some "sea of glass, mingled with fire."

Though far from being insensible to the charms of music, yet no concert of human voices ever thrilled me half so much as the morning or the evening piping of the thrush, in some greenwood glen, where the living waters of some gushing stream mingled its voice in the melody, or the lark warbling his song of love and gladness far up on the great glowing arch of the rainbow. The cuckoo's soft monotonous lay ever delights me more than the sweetest sound of any lute ; and not even the dismal wail of the coronach, in the rocky Highlands, could fill my heart with such a feeling of strange sorrow and sadness, as does the bleeting of a flock of newly weaned lambs away out in some wild glen among the steep green pastoral hills. I have mentioned these things, in order to account for the very little allusion which I make in my poems to cities or to city life ; or to the manners and customs of mankind in their busy and populous haunts. With these I am unfamiliar; and of them, therefore, I have never tried to sing. Among the hills I am most at home, and always, when opportunity presents itself, I delight in saying to myself in these glowing and unsurpassed lines of your own matchless song of " Summer " :—

" Hie away to the vale through whose bosom the wave
     Of the cool water flows, where the heated kine lave ;
     Where the linden and rowan sprays stoop down to drink,
     And the snowy-belled lotus reclines on the brink !
     O Iris-robed Summer ! the queen of the year !
     All Nature is jocund when thou dost appear ;
     The lark hymns thy praise through the long hours of light,
     And the nightingale sings by thy couch all the night ;
     'Tis merry, 'tis merry in greenwood and glen,
     For the sunny-eyed Summer is come back again."

It has been the contemplation of scenes like these, and of those kindred to them, that has ever made me sing; and I sang, because thus gazing on the varied, boundless, and beautiful fields of Nature made my heart to overflow.

How I have succeeded, and how I have managed the thirteen legitimate though different measures in which I have sung "The Circling Year," I must now leave you and the world to judge. To me, however, it will always be a source of unmingled pleasure, that I have dedicated this volume to one who has so long occupied a foremost and an enduring place in the literature of our country; whose poems are as pure as they are sweet, and filled with all that constitutes the truest and highest poetic genius; while your prose writings are characterised by a classic purity of style, surpassing power, melting pathos, poetic splendour, sparkling wit, and rare originality of thought.

That you may be long spared to adorn still further the fields of literature, to be an honour to your country, and a benefactor of mankind, is the sincerest wish of,

DEAR DR WALLER,

Your admiring Friend,

A. B. TODD.

BREEZYHILL COTTAGE, CUMNOCK,
AYRSHIRE, 31st *July* 1880.

NTRODUCTION.

TO sing the Seasons as in months they roll,
    I fain would try, would some muse favour me;
How great storms waste the earth beyond control
Of proud though puny man. How winds set free
From hidden caves, career along the sea,
Stranding strong navies, as the big storms yell,
On to th' affrighted land; where leafless tree
Crashes to earth, as the wild tempests swell
Through the dark winter months, o'er mountain,
    moor, and dell.

How April brings the glad glints of the Spring;
How budding May comes in her garments green,
When streams make music, and the small birds sing,
How June with rose and daisy decks the scene,
Weaving her garlands like a fairy screen;
How July brings the fertilising shower,

Lading the leafy trees with silver sheen;
How bounteous August, in the thunder's power,
Speaks to the earth from heav'n, and gilds the mid-
    night hour.

To tell how Ceres' horn, high fill'd, runs o'er,
As rich September swells all hearts with joy;
Heaping with golden grain the threshing-floor,
Brought from the field by brown-faced farmer's boy,
To whom October suns bring small alloy,
Though pale they glimmer on the yellow trees;
And merry larks morn's hours no more employ,
To pour their music on the mountain breeze,
Nor heard at gloamin' now, the hum of home-bound
    bees.

I, too, may tell, when comes November dun,
How storms assail the fast-expiring year,
And sullen clouds obscure the wan cold sun;
And midnight meteors awe mankind with fear,
As blood-red streamers their battalions rear
High in the air, where shot-stars madly rush,
Flaming through heav'n, and to the earth draw near,

As if man and his boasted works to crush,
And in dark chaos' realms, his voice for ever hush.

December, dull and drear, will close the scene—
Cheerless these days which see its sun-blinks short;
Fast fly the seasons, and the years, I ween,
Are shorter now than when, at playful sport,
I tripp'd the green in life's gay opening court.
What days of light and shadow pass'd away
Since then, when now, with quiet sober port,
I pace the road to where light's every ray
Is quench'd by death, till dawns the everlasting day.

JANUARY.

WHEN Janus* brings the new-born year,
The day is short, the sky is drear;
The joyous laugh may rend the air,
The sparkling goblet mock at care;
And where the merry bands convene,
All may forget the outward scene;
Yet now, where all was late so fair
With flow'r and fruit, now all is bare;
And in the cold frost's killing grasp,
The earth is bound, while wide is cast
A snowy shroud o'er hill and dale,
While streamlets straying in the vale,
Their brawling, bickering sound give o'er;
E'en waterfalls forget to roar,

---

* The god of the year in Roman mythology, to whom the first
day was sacred, and in whose honour it was celebrated with
riotous feasting and giving of presents.

And living flood, in every stream,
Seems sinking into sleepy dream;
As high upon the cascade's brink,
The frost-bound waters cease to sink
Into the caldron far beneath,
Where all is silent now as death;
For steamy vapour, foamy bell,
Upon the pool have ceased to swell;
And in the tangled copsewood bare,
No sound of living thing is there,
Save robin piping on some spray,
Frost-glittering in the sun's brief ray,
Which, faint and low, in southern sky,
Scarce o'er the hill-top lifts his eye.

Now far among the louring clouds
The Spirit of the Storm him shrouds.
At first afar, and moaning low,
The howling hurricane lets go;
Soon all around, in wrathful mood,
It rends the forest, swells the flood;
When rains descend and hailstones rattle,
As if Heaven's hosts had join'd in battle.

Hoarse shrieks the wind 'mong mountain caves,]
And demon-like o'er moorland raves,
Afar, old Ocean in his wrath
Leaps high beneath the tempest's breath,
Which sweeps the waste of waters o'er,
And breaks the tall ships on the shore;
Yells loud along the beetling coast,
While far the billows' foam is toss'd.

On such a night, long, dark, and chill,
When snow-blasts whistled round the hill—
When, through dense clouds, fierce bolts of flame
From out th' Almighty's quiver came
And glared afar, while crash'd the thunder—
In winter thought " a world's wonder "—
When stifling snowdrift hurried past
Upon the blinding mountain blast;
When living thing could scarcely breathe
Upon that broad and blasted heath,
Which stretches from Cairntable grey
To where Ayr winds its infant way
Westward through Airsmoss, wild and lone,
Where pious pilgrims seek the stone

Where saintly Richard Cameron's blood
Flow'd on the heath in crimson flood,
When bloody bigots ruled the land
By gun, and spear, and gleaming brand:
A shepherd o'er the treacherous moor
Sought through the drift his cottage door.
Close round his face his plaid he drew,
As with strong step he struggled through
The thick'ning drift and snowy wreath
Which fill'd each mossy hag beneath.
Along the moor no single ray
Of light shone down to point the way;
Or when at times the lightning shone,
His landmarks on the moor were gone.
Wistful he gazed to catch the light
Which from his cot in winter night
Stream'd far along the level wild
From hearth, round which his dear ones smiled.
He strain'd his eye, but not a glare
Of light could pierce the dark, dense air.
Full oft he thought his home was near,
And oft upon his listening ear
He thought he heard his young wife's cry

Come on the hoarse blast hurrying by ;
'Twas fancy all, he thought, then pale
With fear, his heart began to fail.
What, if he died upon the wild,
Would Marion do, and his dear child ?
That thought gave strength, he struggled on,
But starts to hear a long, deep groan
Close to the place where Piper led—
His faithful dog—which turn'd its head,
Whined in his face, fawn'd and stood still ;
When quavering cry came sharp and shrill
Through the dense air, nor far away ;
When, faint, he sees a flickering ray
Gleam through a momentary rift
Which open'd in the cloudy drift.
Quick, stooping down where Piper stood,
He found what froze his warm heart's blood—
His young wife buried in the snow,
With bosom cold and frozen brow.
In agony he bore her on
To where the red light glimmering shone ;
His good dog bounding on before,
Unto his own dear cottage door.

The embers on the hearth burn'd low;
But soon to him the brightest glow—
The light of life in Marion's eye—
Beam'd out, and turn'd to baby's cry,
Where from his side, as sound he slept,
The mother from his crib had crept
To list the coming of his sire;
When, stumbling in a deep quagmire,
While storm and drift raved all around,
Long had she sought, but never found
Her way back to her infant's bed,
So in the snowstorm reel'd her head;
Her senses gone before he woke,
His cry her deep swoon never broke.

The storm raged on, the cottage shook,
But psalms from out the Holy Book
Were sung by them for mercy given,
And pierced, with prayer, the stormy heaven.

FEBRUARY.

WHEN streamlets wail in icy mail,
    And down the dun rocks trickle,
And cutting gale sweeps through the vale,
    Comes February fickle.

Viewless below, the strong winds blow,
    Along the bleak earth roaring ;
And swollen streams go with dashing flow,
    Down to the ocean pouring.

Yet length'ning day, and strength'ning ray
    Of sunshine soft and cheery,
Now surely say, that soon away
    Will fly the winter dreary.

And now is seen, on cottage green,
    The crocus brightly gleaming ;
And oft between in woody dean,
    The snowdrop pure is beaming.

When the south wind the lakes unbind,
   And rippling rills run gladly,
Winter unkind we leave behind,
   When earth looks wan and sadly.

Behind the plough the peasant now,
   Below the high hills hazy,
With thoughtless brow sends ploughshare through
   Spring's first sweet bright-eyed daisy.

Blithe as a bee along the lea,
   With team all strong and steady,
At morn him see from care all free,
   The corn bed making ready

For March winds dry, when dust clouds fly
   Round sober sower pacing ;
While far on high, across the sky,
   The dull cold clouds are racing.

The clear moonbeam glows on the stream
   All night, and on the mountains,
And wood fays dream, as glad orbs gleam
   By night, on quiet fountains.

Each twinkling star in heaven afar,
  Down in the blue lakes gleaming,
Shows not a scar of sin to mar
  Its angel beauty beaming.

Oft through these nights " the northern lights "
  Round the wide sky are flashing;
When peasant wights see in such sights
  Heaven's hosts to battle dashing;

Or presage sure, that soon shall pour
  Blood in dread torrents streaming;
And wild war roar on many a shore,
  And earth with woes be teeming.

Now fresh winds play at dawn of day,
  And living streams are laving
The banks yet grey, where budding spray
  Of " silver saugh " is waving.

Though often pale on cutting gale,
  The snowflake fierce is flying,
And rough winds wail, o'er hill and dale,
  Through leafless forests sighing.

Then silent fly the ravens by
　When night comes lone and louring,
To pine-wood high, where sadly sigh
　Tempests and torrents pouring.

Or sailing low to some bare bough
　Of forest monarch rocking;
As hailstones go the branches through
　He perches, cawing, croaking.

And robin red there lifts his head,
　Though loud the storm is raging;
Though day is fled, and night's pall spread,
　In song he is engaging.

Yet in the night, the moonbeams bright
　Through rent clouds oft come peering;
And on the sight the starry light
　Breaks as the day is nearing.

A peaceful hush ere morning blush—
　Or as the day is breaking
With rosy flush—wakes up' the thrush
　To Spring's first merry-making.

Then glad is made the winding glade
  By this first wildwood singing,
Nor long delay'd, in mountain shade,
  We wait the lark's song ringing.

My natal time! my heart-strings chime
  To Spring's voice, or the braying—
In our cold clime—of storm sublime,
  Which much to me are saying.

Of my own fate, of love and hate,
  Of fortune changeful ever,
Of which we prate in every state
  While sailing down Time's river.

Ah! where lies now my mother's brow,
  Once o'er her fond babe bending?
It lies full low, where gowans grow,
  But God, His angels sending,

Shall make the graves heave like wild waves,
  And rouse the long, long sleepers
'Neath clay, from caves where ocean raves,
  Where ne'er stood woe-wan weepers!

That sweet-toned tongue which o'er me sung,
  And pray'd with me at even,
Dull death has stung, though she has strung
  Her glad harp in high heaven.

There now on high, with waiting eye,
  Her better self undying;
Without a sigh sees her clay lie,
  The ransom day descrying.

O mother dear! thou canst not hear
  Thy son in sore strife sighing,
For in thine ear heaven's harpings clear
  Drown sorrow's deepest crying.

O! may I dare by faith and pray'r,
  To reach thy star-gemm'd dwelling;
With angels there, to breathe the air
  Of blessedness excelling.

MARCH.

'TIS March, and whistling through the dell
    The winds go piping sharp and shrill,
And wave the osiers round the well,
    Which feeds the brooklet of the hill.

Far o'er the wild the plovers wail,
    Along the lea the lapwings call,
And skylarks briskly sing and sail
    Up o'er the clouds till evening's fall.

By shelter'd bank and briery brake,
    When shadows lengthen on the green,
And sinking sunbeams gild the lake,
    The chirming partridge oft is seen.

When golden beams glint o'er the hills,
    And stars grow pale as day returns,
His morning song the mavis trills,
    And in the wood the ringdove mourns.

Now, landward, sea-gulls stretch their wings,
   Though north winds wail along the wild,
And far the boom of bittern rings
   Round lone marsh, scaring mountain child.

Wide, wheeling round, the curlew screams,
   And lures the wand'rer from its nest,
And far out in sequester'd streams
   The solemn heron bathes its crest.

Still sings the robin on the thorn,
   That grows close by the cottage door;
There children scatter crumbs at morn,
   And weep when there he sings no more.

There, often at the window-pane,
   When winter storms obscure the sky,
He taps, till summer smiles again,
   When to love-making far he'll fly,

Off to the lone streams murmuring through
   The deepest, densest, forests green;
Where scarce heaven's bright expanse of blue
   Can smile in through the leafy scene.

When withering winds have dried the soil,
  Which frosts have fructified before,
Then gladly does the sower toil,
  Hoping for harvest heaps in store.

Behind him see the happy boy
  All day the rattling harrows guide ;
And oft in song the hours employ,
  Which slow and tedious seem to glide.

'Tis spring with him, as with the year,
  And gleams of a glad summer time
Break on his sight, with manhood near,
  But not his sear leaf, past its prime.

In boyhood how we sigh to reach
  The glory and the strength of man,
Impatient when the greyhair'd preach,
  Of life's path full of spectres wan ;

Of blasted hopes, of short-lived joys,
  Of friendships false, or slander riven ;
Of love with dark and dim alloys—
  All lost for which we most have striven.

As o'er the sea of life we sail,
  Our course we heed not for a while,
Until we hear the anguish wail,
  From Time's far shore, where breakers boil.

Where Death, grim pilot, guides each bark,
  Where shipwreck seizes every crew,
Where on th' impenetrable dark
  No sun a radiance ever threw.

How vast the gulf, how deep the grave,
  Where enter all the tribes of men,
Where death's dread billows ever rave,
  Where Spring light never gleams again!

The Seasons circle, and the Spring
  Returns with each returning year,
But life, upon its waving wing,
  Brings only one brief spring-time here.

But yet, heav'n-lighted, in the soul
  A ray divine for ever beams,
And speaks death not the final goal
  It to our mortal vision seems.

On the dark clouds around the tomb,
   We read, in bright celestial ray,
That man, God's offspring, yet shall bloom
   In the fair fields of endless day.

There, in the light of God, to live,
   When stars sink in eternal night;
When suns, unseated, no more give
   To boundless space their rosy light.

Philosophy marks not the road
   On to this land of endless spring,
Which lies far round the throne of God,
   Where life's pure waters flow and sing.

But Christ, in His triumphant war,
   Has clear'd the path and points the way;
His conquering banner streams afar,
   And leads to everlasting day.

Who would not, then, beneath it go,
   Who would not trust th' eternal Word,
And gladly bear the cross below,
   To gain the mansions of the Lord?

No frosts shall blast the blossoms there,
　Which flourish on the " Tree of Life ; "
But flower and fruit, for ever fair,
　Monthly, upon that tree are rife.

On, then, my soul, through grief and pain ;
　On from earth's low allurements go ;
And let not honour, love, or gain
　Bind thy hopes to this world below.

APRIL.

'TIS April, and brighter the sun
 Beams down through the blue veil of heaven
Upon woods, where glad rivulets run,
 Where the birds are all vocal at even;
Where now in each glen, grassy green,
 The cowslip and primrose appear,
With the daisy and pansy between,
 Smiling up to the spring of the year.

When the morning comes red o'er the hills,
 Where the winds wander gentle and free,
And the music of lone mountain rills
 Comes wafted by turret and tree;
Then a voice, soft and sweet, gushes forth
 From the bud-swelling tree, or the wall
Of the ivy-bound ruin—on earth
 Few sounds can the heart so enthral

As the cuckoo, which gaily is calling,
 And filling the glen with its note,

Where the sound of the clear water falling
    Swells the breeze by the straw-cover'd cot.
Shy bird of the mountain and glen,
    Of the ruin and old scroggy tree;
The eye brightens to hear thee again,
    Passing round the wide world far and free.

When the days of the month are well over,
    Its smiles and its tears nearly run;
Then, blithely, another sweet rover
    Comes swift from the climes of the sun.
The rude blust'ring winds of brown autumn
    Had warn'd him away from our shore;
For the great Lord of nature had taught him
    To fly from our winter's wild roar.

O swallow! how sweet is thy twitter,
    By the window and brown shelving brae;
And how subtly the young sunbeams glitter
    On thy wing, as thou skimmest thy way
O'er the blue stream that sings through the valley,
    O'er the lake 'mid the circling hills,

Where the thunderbolts gather and rally,
   Where the rivers are narrow'd to rills.

There, afar, in these dread chambers grim,
   Where the thunder holds in its hot breath,
Till, anon, o'er the dun mountain's brim,
   It breathes its fork'd arrows of death.
Then scarce slower thy wing cuts its course
   Through the wide yielding waves of the air,
Darting low o'er the bright blooming gorse,
   Nor, in fear, even lingering there;

Till thy home in the eaves thou hast found,
   Of the cottage, the castle, or hall;
Where thy nest turns the lightning around,
   Or pass harmless, and strike not at all. *
When the roll of the thunder is over,
   And the blinding glare comes not again,
Then, gladly, thou leavest thy cover,
   And skimmest away through the glen;

---

* It has been a long and a widespread opinion that no thunder-
bolt will break where the sweet and harmless swallow builds its
nest.

Where, on gowan, and fresh springing grass,
    Hang the raindrops like diamonds bright;
And away up the green mountain pass,
    Where the lambkins are racing in sight;
While, softly, the blue sky of heaven
    Bends its arch o'er the beautiful scene,
And soft, on the light winds of even,
    Comes the psalm song of shepherd serene.

Away through the rim of the rainbow,
    Bathing deep in its beautiful light,
The swift little bird is aglow,
    In its colours as dazzling and bright
As the bow which the rapt banish'd seer,
    Of old in the lone Patmos isle,
Saw encircle the throne in that sphere
    Where the saints ever bask in its smile.

Now calm sinks the sun o'er the mountains
    Away in the isles of the west,
In whose clear, lovely, rippling fountains
    His last look, at evening, is cast.
The hum of the hamlet grows silent,
    The songs of the birds die away,

And the rush of the river, less vi'lent,

    Seems to whirl round the cascade in spray.

Far down in the valley, the wood

    Looms dark in the lingering light,

Where, for ages, the elm-trees have stood

    Round the home of the dead, now in sight.

There the low, plaintive dirge of the river

    Sounds on as the seasons go by;

But none of the long sleepers ever

    Send back a response or a sigh.

There the blithe lark has welcomed the morn

    Through the long circling seasons of spring;

And, though sweet pipes the thrush from the thorn,

    Yet the dead are all deaf while they sing.

The roar of wild storm has rush'd by;

    Earth was awed at the terrible blast;

And the thunders of God in the sky

    Have shook the strong hills settled fast.

Yet dull the dead ears to them all—

    To the voices of nature or man,

But they'll start when the archangel's call
  Round the far fields of ether has run ;
When the earth, which has now waxen old,
  Shall be changed by a heavenlier spring;
When strong angels, with harps of bright gold,
  Make the depths of immensity ring.

Then the sore wounds of sin and its sorrow,
  Shall be heal'd by the hand of the Lord,
And no dread of calamitous morrow
  Cast a gloom over Eden restor'd.
Then the winter of death shall be over,
  And its darkness, which hid friends from view;
Then the lost babe shall find its fond mother,
  And mankind their friendships renew.

MAY.

O H, sweet is the light balmy breath of the morn,
    When May opens its eye on the earth;
When the bees cluster thick on the snowy-white thorn,
    And the lambs race the meadows in mirth;
When the young birds, 'mid music, are brought into
        birth,
    In the hedgerows and trees, leafy green;
When the drowsy kine browse on the gowany brae,
And the lark full of joy sings up and away,
Afar through the dappled clouds, golden and grey,
    O! pleasant the prospect, I ween.

The corn-craik is creaking in green clover field,
    At the foot of the mountain so still,
Where the shepherd at noonday his senses up-yield
    To meek Morpheus' care-soothing will;
Though the sunbeams dart down o'er the brow of the
        hill
    Upon him with vehement heat,

Yet, lull'd by the cuckoo's melodious lay,
And the wind wailing low o'er the green-springing hay,
He heeds not the heat, nor how time glides away,
   More than sheep nibbling round at his feet.

By the brink of the burn the bright yellow broom
   Hangs its flowers o'er the green linnet's nest,
And all round the hill, where the gay bushes bloom,
   Song swells each bird's loving breast;
As he sings to his mate from the green mountain's
     crest,
   Where, close by the rivulet clear,
She spreads her warm wings o'er her young callow
     brood,
Protects them from cold, while the father brings food,
Then sings, when they're fill'd, by the verge of the
     wood,
   Her long hours of watching to cheer.

High o'er the pine forest, which frowns on the hill,
   The ravens wheel round with hoarse cry,
Which mingles discordant with voice of the rill
   Which brightly goes rippling by

The bow'rs where, at evening, the young lovers sigh,
   When the hawthorn is scenting the vale,
As the last sunbeams fall on the lake broad and bright,
And the soft murm'ring waters to musing invite,
And the clouds of the sky in the fair saffron-light
   Scarcely stir with the slow moving gale.

Now the gay apple bow'rs, in the star-lighted even,
   Distil their sweet balm on the breeze,
As the moon rides on high, in the calm, dewy heaven,
   Gleaming down through the green trembling trees,
Where all sights and all sounds seem created to please,
   And pluck from the heart carking care—
In the soft, tender mind heal the pains of the past,
While the beacons of hope a glad radiance cast
On the path of Time's chariot, unstaying and fast,
   Gliding on to the future, so fair.

Round the lawn the laburnums wave gaudy and bright
   In the breath of the soft summer air,
And away where the level mead comes into sight,
   The buttercups gleam everywhere;
While far up on high, in the cloudlets so fair,

The lark sings to his love on the green,
Where the white gowan smiles, like a star on the lea,
And the daffodil bends to the big humble bee,
And the butterfly sports all around in its glee,
    Till sweet gloamin' draws on its grey screen.

When the sunbeams were drinking morn's dew from
        the flowers
    Far out in the clefts of the hill;
And the winds wanton'd light in the sweet birchen
        bowers,
    By the banks of the babbling rill;
And the wail of the plover rang mournful and shrill,
    Away o'er the wide level waste;
A shepherd's wee lassie look'd up in his face,
Then came to his knee, with a bound and a race,
Though some wondering awe in her eye he could
        trace,
    As thus she began in her haste:—

"O father, I dreamt in a strange land I stood,
    By the brink of a slow sluggish stream;

I safely had cross'd, yet though how, the dark flood,
  I never could find in my dream.
Behind all was dim, but before me a beam
  Of glory play'd far o'er the fields,
Where flowers flourish'd fairer than those round our
    well—
The lilies so white—where the bees love to dwell,
While full on my ear far sweeter sounds fell,
  Than our evening psalm ever yields.

" In sorrow and sadness, I thought you stood there,
  Away in the gloom, o'er the wave;
You gazed on me long, till with terrified stare,
  Your eye settled down on a grave.
I saw you in fear, though I knew you were brave;
  I was awed at your now feeble form,
At the stream of salt tears which you bitterly shed,
At the sighs which you heaved o'er that low grassy bed,
At the dark bushy locks turning white on your head,
  Like a fir in a fierce snowy storm.

" I look'd at you long; but your eye caught not me,
  Though I stood on a heaven-lighted shore;

Where bright forms sung under each fair branchy
   tree—
I was charm'd as I ne'er was before.
I lifted my eyes, the strange scene to explore,
   When, astonish'd, there burst on my view
A temple afar, on a fair mountain height:
In size it was vast, it was shining and bright,
It seem'd girdled with gold, though, like snow, it was
   white,
   And no shadow of night it e'er knew.

" Hands, soft and unseen, soon bore me away
   To that temple of light in the sky,
Where, though no sun I saw, yet the brightness of
   day
Glow'd down through the palms waving high.
How I thought of you, Father, and wish'd you were
   nigh ;
   For who should come smiling to me,
But Mother, dear Mother ! whom death took so late,
Whom we wept for so long, and mourn'd our hard fate,
O ! how lovely she look'd at that fair temple gate,
   Now from sorrow and suffering free.

C

" The bands of sleep broke at the joy that I felt
  To meet my sweet mother once more ;
I sigh'd when I woke, for I aye could have dwelt
  With the saints on that sorrowless shore ;
But we'll pass to her yet, though the sad sullen roar
  Of Death's river lies broad in our way ;
For the Angels of God are ever at hand,
To divide the dark flood with a wave of their wand,
And guide us all safe to Immanuel's land—
  Fair land of unwearied day."

The sunbeams of ev'ning stream'd up from the west,
  And the shadows stretch'd far o'er the green,
The last purple rays kiss'd the high mountain's crest,
  And fairy-like colour'd the scene ;
May was closing its course with its holiest mien,
  As the shepherd came home from the hill,
His thoughts were of Mary, who kiss'd him at morn,
Whose dream fill'd his heart, now of peacefulness
    shorn,
When, there, bounding on, by the milky white thorn,
  His lassie leapt light o'er the rill.

Half gliding in air, like a fairy in flight,
    Afar on a beam of the moon,
She waved her white hands, while her amber hair
        bright
Glow'd like a glad sunbeam at noon.
All eager to meet her, and clasp her so soon,
    He paced the green lea fast and light.
He saw her fall forward, then wildly wheel round:
Did she melt in the air? did she sink in the ground?
He leapt o'er the rill, gain'd the height at a bound,
    But his Mary had vanish'd from sight.

They sought her within, and they sought her without,
    And wildly they call'd on her name;
They sought her in bushes and hollows about,
    But the dear one nor answer'd, nor came.
With a wild wail of woe, and a trembling frame,
    Down the garden the father has sped
To where the green bushes surrounded the well;
The branches, all broken, proclaim'd where she fell—
There, with lily in hand, I mournful must tell,
    The dear little maiden was dead!

JUNE.

'TIS June, leafy June, and the wild roses blow,
   And soft through the vales the streams murmur
      and flow,
Where the shy little wren, in the brow of the brae,
Has its nest hidden well from the glare of the day;
Where the trees overhead, with their roots in the rock,
Hold their tops to the sky in the storm's rudest shock;
Though now in the glad waters wimpling past,
Their long pliant arms o'er the bright flood are cast,
While their green leaves are kissing the clear crystal
      wave
Which coyly whirls on past the cool rocky cave,
Where, lull'd by the river's melodious tune,
The boys love to stay through the long afternoon;
While, close at their feet, the glad waters lave,
And the light sparkling foam-bells invite them to
      bathe,

Till the last fringe of daylight is leaving the hill,

And down o'er the earth steals the ev'ning still,

When, nearing the hill-tops, the sun bends him low,

And the clouds following after are all in a glow

Of glory and gold, as around him they lie,

Like couches of angels, afar in the sky;

While the peaks of the mountains all flicker with fire,

And a saffron light plays round the grey village spire;

And the woods of the west in the soft mellow light,

Wave a smiling farewell to the sun for the night;

And the briar-rose laughs up to the last beam of day—

Oh! how fast it will shed in his fierce noontide ray;

Like the brief hours of pleasure, which thrill in the
 heart,

When play'd on by sorrow, how soon they depart.

Now the dusk sends each truant boy off to his home,

Through the vales, where the fleecy flocks nibble and
 roam ;

As the night winds sigh faintly on moorland and hill,

And sweeter from far comes the song of the rill,

Which never is silent, but sings evermore,

Though leaving its banks for eternity's shore.

Go the old and the young, the parent and child,

To the dim spirit-land, from their homes in the wild;

For the passions of youth bring the frailties of age,

Though here all move calmly on life's narrow stage.

But the stream, ever young, still sings down the dell,

As glad as when first o'er its cascades it fell.

Shall the time ever come when its song, too, is past,

And its last soothing sigh on the night air is cast?

Shall the starlight be darken'd afar in the heaven,

And the spheres by the archangel's trumpet be riven?

Shall the sun lose his lustre, and reel in the sky, ·

And the blood-smitten moon in astonishment die?

Yes, that dread time shall come, when the ages have

    roll'd,

Which the prophets in vision have seen and foretold;

With the new heaven they sang of aglow in the sky,

While, bathed in its glory, beneath it shall lie

A new earth, rejoicing, immortal and young,

Which out of the wreck of the old shall have sprung;

Where the glad stream of life shall murmur and play

Past the palm-trees of Eden, for ever and aye;

Where the dwellers shall walk with the angels of God,
And never wax old on eternity's road.

The night is departing, the short night of June,
Morn kindles the hill-tops, the birds are atune;
The glad beams of morning now scatter the gloom,
And the sleeping winds wake on their beds of perfume;
The lark on the green turf has open'd his eye,
And soars away singing, till lost in the sky;
The cuckoo calls gaily on old ivy tow'r,
And the thrush pipes his love song in green birchen
    bow'r;
The bee leaves her cell with the morn's rosy glow,
And hies her away where the sweetest flow'rs blow;
The heathcock is whirring afar on the moor,
And the milch kine low up to the dairyman's door,
Where the blue smoke goes curling high up in the air,
To mix with the light fleecy clouds floating there;
While the silver dew shines upon daisy and rose,
And all flow'rs which the gay cultured gardens disclose;
And the blooming shrubs blush on the lovely parterre;
While around all is beauty and peace everywhere;

Yet man comes abroad, with a cloud on his brow,

And the deep lines of sorrow from care's scathing plough;

For the beauty of earth, and the fair spangled heaven,

Can heal not, though soothing, the heart sorrow-riven.

The morning is over, and high rides the sun,

And half of his circle through heaven has been run;

The sky has been clear, and the air has been still,

But dense clouds now are frowning afar o'er the hill;

Spread a pall o'er the wood, and a gloom on the lake,

While the wind wakes and sighs in strange gusts

    through the brake;

On the verge of the heav'n, vapour columns arise,

While a dim weary film o'er the firmament flies;

The great eye of day looks as losing his light,

And the birds all grow mute as at mid-hour of night;

Strange sounds on the mountains moan fitful and far,

And the winds and the waterfalls murmur and jar.

Swelling up o'er the hill tops, the clouds curl on high,

And mingle and whirl on the face of the sky;

Where the red lurid lightning is forming unseen,

Conceal'd from the eye by the thick thunder-screen,

Which stretches from mountain to mountain away,

In silence profound, though its folds swell and sway;

While the stillness of death, now paining the ear,

Awes the heart of the wayfaring pilgrim with fear.

The silence is short, for a quivering gleam

Darts through the dark curtain, and glares on the
stream;

When the pinewood so black seems to blaze in a
fire,

And the lone shaggy hill looks a vast flaming pyre;

And the thunder on high, from his cloud-pillar'd throne,

Comes with crash, and with rattle, and long hollow
groan;

Across the wide arch the storm-curtain is riven,

And the chain bolts leap forth from the black boiling
heaven;

And one earth-rocking peal has not hush'd or grown
still,

Ere a louder has burst o'er the brow of the hill;

While the rainflood and hailstones rush down on the
earth,

As if demons had call'd the dread storm into birth,

And the small rills, like rivers, come down on the plain,
While the broad rivers swell like the storm-smitten
    main.

Away in the wild the thunder's hot breath
Had rent the old ash-tree, and kindled the heath;
Where a little lad tended his flock on the moor,
Afar from his young master's sheltering door.
Who thought of the laddie, all timid and lone,
So away to his aid on the moor he has gone.
He hails him from far, and they both hurry home,
While the thunder is rending heavn's far-flaming dome.

Betrothed to the farmer, fair Helen looks out,
With a fast panting heart, of his safety in doubt;
She sees them come down by the verge of the wood,
While faster to earth fall the fire and the flood;
A wide-spreading oak, with great antlers outcast,
Tempts to stay underneath, till the torrent be past.
A flash, and a crash, with the oak sheathed in flame,
She saw, and she heard, with a palsied frame;
All rush'd to the spot, where a cleft tree they found,

With the little lad safe, but stretch'd on the ground
Young William lay dead, with calm placid face,
Yet no mark and no scar on his form they could trace.
Young Helen, in agony, fainted away;
And, though living, spoke little, till winter was grey.
The spring came again, and the small birds were glad;
Fair summer succeeded, still Helen was sad;
And the circling year, on its swift-wingëd way,
Brought round to fair Helen the sorrowful day ;
Then she sought a lone bow'r, where a burn wimpled
    bye,
Where the fatal spot open'd full out to her eye.
Friends sought her down there, in the still afternoon,
And they thought she sat soothed by the rivulet's tune;
Then they thought her asleep, with the Bible outspread
'Neath her lily-white hands, but dear Helen was dead!

JULY.

THE lingering rays of June's last setting sun
   Have faded from the fringed horizon's verge,
Telling that half the circling year has pass'd,
To join th' eternity which lies behind,
And swallows up the months, yet lessens not
The dread eternity which lies before.

The night wind gently fann'd the leafy trees,
The stars shone faintly in the dreamy sky,
Where the meek silver moon unclouded shone,   .
Shedding her soft beams in upon the stream,
Through trembling trees, sweet rustling on the ear.
With solemn mien, thus gently June departs,
And July now, through her resplendent reign,
Must, at the morn, unbar the gates of light,
And roll away the clouds that nightly hang

Their folds before the portals of the dawn,
And pierce with quivering beams the mists that lie
On moor, and mountain, gorge, and verdant vale,
When by the light winds stirr'd they float along,
And soar with graceful sweep away from view.

With the glad morning joyous voices come
From wood, and brake, and bank of purling stream;
Where all the birds rejoice and sing, though now
Less lustily than when the glad green May
Stretch'd her bright mantle o'er the laughing fields,
Fragrant and lovely with earth's first fair flowers.
Far in among the hills the air is fill'd
With plaintive bleating of the fleecy flocks.
The weaning time has come, and the sweet lambs
Call mournful for their mothers; these again
Give agonising answer from afar,
And the wide hills ring with the piteous wail.
Poor lambs! how short your morning time of joy;
How brief your gambols on the gowany green,
Down by the gushing burn. The spoiler comes—
Your strange protector for a time—and hunts

You from your thymy braes to shambles grim,
To throb and perish 'neath the horrid knife.

The piping breeze, the piercing clarion call
Of stately chanticleer, the morning song
Of the glad lark, warbling away to heav'n,
Soaring and singing in the amber cloud;
Or, out of sight, above the rainbow's rim,
Wake men and women, dreaming on their beds
Of plans and plottings, poverty and wealth;
Of love's successful suits, of blasted hopes,
And call them forth to life's perpetual battle,
Each morn begun, yet every night unended.

Now wheeling in his chariot, up the sun
Rides round the path so oft in glory gone,
Pouring refulgent beams, through thin white clouds,
From the blue bending sky on the wide scene
Stretch'd out beneath—on the lone heathy wild,
And hoary mountains, whose grey jagged peaks
Pierce the cerulean vault; on crystal pool,
Where trailing osiers fringe the purling brook;

On waterfall, deep in some hidden dell,
Where honeysuckle and the wild briar-rose,
With prickly eglantine, diffuse their sweets.
Bright glow the cornfields in the golden beams;
The gardens glitter, and the meadows smile,
Where maidens, making hay, with gladness sing
Behind the mowers bending o'er their scythes,
With simultaneous swing, harmonious sweep,
Laying the long green grass in ridgy swathes.
Bright undecaying sun! undimm'd thou shin'st,
Unsullied, young, serene as when at first
Thy glorious rays stream'd on the new-born earth,
Which to perfection sprang at God's command—
A wondrous work of high Almighty Power—
When all the heavenly host admiring sang
Strains which went echoing in among the stars
In loud acclaim, till, through creation vast,
Adoring hallelujahs rang to God!

July, sweet month! meridian of the year!
The fields rejoice in thy life-giving beams,
The yellowing grain looks glad, the luscious fruit

In the gay gardens blushes in the sun,

And mellows in the pale light of the moon;

And where the tow'ring plane-trees line the banks

Of the clear stream, or wave in the wide park,

The bees buzz briskly on the clustering blooms,

Sucking sweet honey through the sunny hours.

'Twas in this month of promise and of hope,

On a mild afternoon, two lovers met

To join a pleasure party, where the Ayr

Looks loveliest through all its lovely course.

The air was calm and still, though on the hills,

Which swell'd all round the west, a dreamy haze

Was resting; and the saffron-colour'd clouds,

With orange mix'd, seem'd melting 'mong the trees,

Which gently quiver'd in the soft south wind,

Which slowly wanton'd through the deep green wood.

As on they wander'd by the bending banks

Of the bright stream which brawl'd far underneath,

Round dizzying rocks which rose high o'er the flood,

And turn'd a wood-crown'd height, and came in view

Of a gay group light tripping on the green

And whirling in the mazes of the dance;
Fair Phœbe started, stood, grew pale, and fear
Look'd from her light blue eyes. Her trembling hand
Her William took in haste, and round her waist
Quick drew his arm. " What ails my love," he said,
" Or what disturbs her thoughts? Here on this knoll
Be seated and composed, and say the cause
Of this thy sudden fear and troubled mien."
The sweat stood thickly on her pale brent brow,
As with quick breath she turn'd to him and said—
" Whence come the dreams that visit us by night?
For surely now they show us things to come.
Here have I never, never been before,
Yet last night, in a dream, I saw this place—
All that I see at present—yon gay group
On the green height, above the beetling rock,
And all yon hills which glow down in the west.
I heard the music, too, which now I hear,
To which these dancers move. I heard the sigh
Of these same waters, murmuring far below.
I thought you pass'd me swiftly; when a wail
Of wildest anguish fell upon my ear;
That broke my sleep, and drove away my dream.

D

I had forgotten all, till now the whole
In strange reality stands full in view.

With some confused, but yet consoling words,
Young William led her onward.   For a time
They eyed the dance, and heard the light love
    song,
And for a while, they were spectators only;
But joy, like grief, infects the looker-on:
Phœbe grew first composed, then happy look'd,
Then, with her lover, join'd the giddy dance,
And whirl'd with him through the bewild'ring waltz,
Until the westering sun, all dazzling bright,
Wheel'd down behind the hills, and twilight dews
Cool'd the hot earth.

                        But one dance more, and then
Off to their homes with gladness they would go.
Phœbe look'd fair as the new-risen moon;
And bright her lover look'd, as ev'ning star
Which smiled and sparkled in the western heaven.
The music ceased, they loosed their love-lock'd grasp,
But as they did, love and the dizzy dance

Made William's brain reel round.　His arms he
　　stretch'd,
Then staggering, whirl'd across the dew-damp green.
An anguish cry came from the cliff's dread verge;
A moment more—a dead, dull, heavy splash
Was heard far down below; when hast'ning there,
They found him mangled in the shallow stream,
With life all gone; and, as the water pass'd
The place he lay, on its unstaying course,
The moonbeams show'd it had a crimson hue!

We may not mention what young Phœbe did,
Or how she look'd, or what she said, or thought:
He suffer'd but a moment, she long years;
He loved her only in the world below,
She longs to join him in the world above.

AUGUST.

'TIS now the busy, bounteous, autumn time;
  The months move round, the year is in its
   prime;
The August breezes bend the ripening grain,
And lightly play along the rippling main;
The giant trees, through all the forest green,
Wave in the sultry winds with languid mien;
The bluebells kiss the streamlets as they flow,
Laughing and tinkling, as they gladly go
To join the rivers sweeping to the sea,
Like travellers to the far eternity.

Oft, William, brother, have we traced some stream
When golden August gave its gladsome gleam;
Threaded the forest, climb'd the breezy hill,
And pluck'd the harebells by the mountain rill;
On shelving rock, by musical cascade,
A fragrant seat upon the wild thyme made;

With raptured eye there view'd the rainbow's rim
Spanning the vales between the mountains dim;
Traversed the moors, where bloom'd the heather-bell
O'er honey treasure, in the wild bee's cell;
And far down in sweet Lugar's lovely glen,
Made Israel's Psalms roll on the breeze again,
Or ring within the Covenanter's cave
(Whose time-worn steps the living waters lave),
And thought of Peden, and his weary life,
True to his God 'mid scoffers, blood, and strife;
Who, when day dawn'd, came here with weary feet
Unmurmuringly, and sought this lone retreat;
Chanting these strains, which Judah's King of old
Harp'd to his God in Engedi's stronghold,—
" Thou art my hiding place, and thou shalt me
From trouble keep, from danger set me free."
Wrestling with God, he pass'd the hours away,
While his rapt eye pierced the far future day;
Then, when on earth the darkness settled down,
And thunderclouds closed in with awful frown,
Grasping his staff, when storm blasts whistled shrill,
And nimble lightnings play'd around the hill,
Would hie him far to some lone desert place,

Known only to the persecuted race;
And there with winning words would point the way
To peace and rest, beyond life's troubled day;
Yet show how wicked men, and foes of God,
To ruin rush'd by many an evil road.

O say not now, when liberty is ours,
And we sit safely in our peaceful bowers,
That these, our fathers, who for freedom fought,
And with their lives our liberties have bought,
Were bigots, and like fools wrought their own death,
And for mere trifles yielded up their breath.
In things divine they nobly would but own
Messiah on His universal throne.
To earthly king they render'd what was his,
And to heaven's Lord would not give less than this.
They bought our freedom with their flowing blood,
When they the tyrant's cruel laws withstood.
These moors oft echoed with the martyrs' moans,
Now studded with their monumental stones;
While, blazon'd on our history's brightest page,
Their fame shall flourish on to latest age.

Oft when the bracing August breezes blew,
We trod the wilds and track'd the valleys through;
On dizzy heights admired the rowans grow,
The clusters mirror'd in the flood below,
Where the glad stream in glassy pools would stay
A little while, then sing its seaward way.
Oft have we linger'd in some upland glen
(The favourite haunt of nature-loving men),
When cooling breezes play'd along the stream,
Bright in the setting sun's last flick'ring beam;
When winds grew hush'd, and umber'd trees stood still,
As gloaming grey crept o'er the eastern hill;
And merry reapers, busy since the morn,
With jocund laugh hied homeward through the corn,
As shone the moon, fair smiling up the east,
And the tall pine-trees seem'd in silver dress'd;
And stars peep'd forth in the blue vault above,
Like angels looking down in silent love;
And earth seem'd answering up in sweetest song
Of living streams, which sigh'd and sung along.

O joyous August! treasure of the year!
I love thee, though thou tell'st of winter near.

Once more I feel myself a boy again,

Heaping with yellow sheaves the groaning wain;

A bright girl cooing round me like a dove,

My heart first fluttering at the touch of love.

That sweet-toned voice, e'en now I seem to hear,

Still sounding sweeter as life's close draws near.

Her rosy lips, bright cheek, and dimpled chin;

Her small round mouth, with faultless teeth within;

Her raven tresses round her shining brow,

Her bright blue eyes (they beam upon me now);

Her heaving breast, tempting as Eden's fruit;

Her slender waist; her small and pretty foot;

All brought a swimming sense upon my brain,

And made my blood career through every vein.

A boy no more; love-lifted, I began

A new life then—in love, a full-grown man!

O! first found, deepest, all unequall'd love!

Though long our lives, and widely though we rove;

Though beauty's fairest daughters flutter round

The paths we tread, warming the dull cold ground;

The soul no more, in their bright dazzling glow,

Flames as when first love's pulse began to go.

That nameless thrill it sends through all the heart
Is ne'er forgotten, nor can quite depart.

But August calls up other thoughts than love,
Thoughts which make all my inmost spirit move.
Whene'er I see the reapers in the corn,
Memory brings back that sorrow-laden morn,
When Death, the dull destroyer, aim'd his dart
Not at my own, but at a Mother's heart.
Fair rose the sun, the day was calm and clear;
All calmly too, she knew the last foe near.
The golden beams play'd round her dying bed,
Bathing in light of heav'n her reverend head.
Closer the spoiler came, his icy breath
She felt, yet calmly whisper'd, " This is death."
In holy psalm she spoke that inward peace
Which grew and brighten'd with her strength's·
    decrease—
" Extol the Lord with me, and let us all
Exalt His name.   He heard me at my call.
The angel of the Lord encamps around
His saints, and they deliverance have found.
O taste with me, and see that God is good;

Who trusts in Him shall not lack heavenly food.
The eyes of God are on the just; His ears
Are ever open, and their cry He hears;
His servants' souls, the Lord redeemeth ever,
And He His saints will leave forsaken never."

With radiant countenance she pass'd away;
That left behind was only breathless clay.
Fast fell our tears, but for ourselves they flow'd,
And her loved guidance on life's perilous road;
Her wise words spoken, and her cheering smile;
Her gentle winning ways, all free from guile.
The light which ever lighten'd her own way,
Show'd us the right, when lured to step astray.

We leave thee, Mother, in the Saviour's smile;
And hope to meet thee in some after while.
O, for thy faith, and hope, and holy will;
Thy brave large heart, under each worldly ill;
That we may go, life's constant battle bye,
To join thee waiting for us in the sky.

September.

A SHORT'NING day, a cooler sun,
  Sober September brings;
And now along the moorland dun
  The grey lark seldom sings,

Or trills a feeble, short-lived lay,
  Where the meandering burn
Sighs ceaseless round the lone green brae
  In many a mazy turn.

Still the bright heather on the hill
  Bends to the busy bee,
Though fainter suns flash on the rill,
  Which wanders far and free.

And blue-bells deck the mossy brook,
  And purple flow'rs the moor,
Where heathcock in some secret nook
  Sips at the rain-drop pure.

The forest birds are silent now,
    A twitter on the tree
We only hear, and to heaven's bow
    No lark soars from the lea.

Few gowans now upon the green
    Smile to the op'ning day;
And wide o'er all the woodland scene
    The fresh green fades away.

Still, in the orchards apples grow,
    All temptingly and red,
On branches waving to and fro,
    High o'er the schoolboy's head.

And near and far some forest tree,
    In gaudy yellow glow,
Gleams in the sun, all fair to see,
    Though soon its pride will go

Away upon the rough wind's breath,
    Which sweeps the hill and dale,
Blasting the wild flow'r on the heath,
    The rose low in the vale.

Upon the bramble, in the brake,
　　The small pale blossoms bloom;
And honeysuckles round the lake
　　Smile through the woodland's gloom.

And cluster'd fair and far on high,
　　Still shine the rowans red,
Where far below the brooklet's sigh
　　Comes from its rocky bed.

Here often now the shy ringdove
　　Coos softly through the glen,
Telling her autumn tale of love,
　　Far out from haunts of men.

All silent now the lapwings fly
　　Along the inland lea,
Ere yet their shoreward way they hie
　　Down to the sounding sea.

And twittering in from airy height
　　To roof of cot or hall,
The dear, sweet swallows thick alight
　　At some strong leader's call;

All, doubtless, holding converse deep
  Of that fast coming day
When they on rapid wing will sweep,
  With straight, unerring way,

To sunny climes, where winter's gloom
  Ne'er gathers o'er the heaven;
Where flow'rs unfading ever bloom,
  And snowstorm never driven.

Now gloriously the harvest moon
  Glows up the eastern sky;
And the bright stars come trooping soon,
  Like lamps hung far on high.

Their silver sheen on streamlet light,
  And on the lake's broad breast;
And through the tall trees glimmer bright,
  And on the mountain's crest.

They glint upon the golden grain,
  Which speaks of plenty near—
Rich treasures spread along the plain,
  To cheer the waning year.

Still, blithe among the yellow corn
  The lads and lasses go;
Making the sheaves since early morn,
  To love's bright bantering flow;

On till the dreamy evening hour,
  When wheels the bat abroad;
When lovers seek the trysting bow'r,
  By lone sequester'd road.

Now is the time of feast and fun—
  The joyous Harvest-home;
Well have they all such pleasure won,
  Long look'd for, now 'tis come.

The sober farmer shares the joy—
  His crop is now secure—
He joins the mirth, lets no alloy
  Mix with the merry hour.

The song rings round, the lightsome dance
  Moves to the music's flow;
The girls' glad smile the lads entrance,
  Blithe gliding as they go.

From near and far the neighbours come
  To join the jovial band;
Some smile in favour'd love, and some
  Rejected, gloomy stand.

Sighing in silent pain to see
  Some maid's averted eye
To rival turn'd, with witching glee,
  Yet his own suit deny.

Such have I seen when life was young,
  And pointed fair and far;
When hope told, with her silver tongue,
  Of joys which nought would jar.

When love stretch'd wide its fairy screen,
  So dazzling to the view,
When not a cloud obscured the scene
  Imagination drew,

Of circling cycles, lengthening far
  Along the vale of years;
All beam'd on by propitious star,
  And all undimm'd by tears.

Still sigh'd we for the future then,
   As now we mourn the past,
And wish our boyhood back again,
   And evermore to last.

This may not be. Nor wealth, nor pow'r,
   Nor pray'rs, nor tears, nor sighs,
Can bring us back the fleeting hour,
   Which comes, glides on, and dies!

And none can stay the noiseless tread
   Of ever-moving time;
Or keep the honours of the head
   Unblanch'd, and in youth's prime.

Still let us pace life's pathway o'er,
   Uneven though it prove,
On to eternity's dread shore,
   In patience, faith, and love.

And bravely bear the ills of life
   (It has its pleasures too),
For though its paths with pains be rife,
   We quickly pass them through.

E

The Heavenly Captain leads us on,
And God's good Spirit guides
To fair realms, round the eternal throne,
Where endless peace abides.

There death shall never wound again,
Nor fears nor sorrow come ;
Nor any sting of burning pain
Hurt in that happy home.

The Captain of the Lord's own host,
Then, let us follow now :
Why turn aside, and so be lost?
Crowns wait each conqueror's brow.

OCTOBER.

OCTOBER'S wan sunlight has yellow'd the trees,
   And gloomy and cold is the dull leaden sky,
And the dry shrivell'd leaves, on the blast and the
    breeze,
   Whirl away with the plaintive wind's murmur and
    sigh.

The storm-cloud rests long on the dark misty moor,
   And wraps the dun hill in a curtain of grey ;
Down the gorge of the mountain the dark torrents pour
   With an eeriesome dash at the close of the day.

The rivers are turbid, and sullenly roar,
   And the grey gelid clouds cast a gloom on the lake ;
And the rills in the moorlands are limpid no more,
   And the lark's song has ceased o'er the far ferny
    brake.

With the presage of winter, the cutting blasts rave
  Afar o'er the wild with a wearisome wail ;
And high up the hill, from the dim rocky cave,
  The croak of the raven comes by on the gale.

The fields now are brown, and look weary and bare,
  The hedges are thin, the old bird-nests are seen,
Though the schoolboy had search'd for, but found them
      not there,
  When the close shelt'ring leaves were new open'd
    and green.

There the ruddy haws hang on the bare prickly thorn,
  Where the robin now sings at the close of the day,
And pipes with clear throat through the cold dreary
    morn,
  When "the flowers of the forest are a' wede away."

On the rough swelling storm-blasts the brown leaves
    sweep by ;
  The stream rushing past bears them on and away ;
Or, trode in the mire, on the highway they lie,
  Their brief beauty vanish'd for ever and aye.

Th' oaks, moss-grown and gnarl'd, round the old ruin
    grey,
Show'r in their sere leaves to the lone roofless hall,
Where the minstrels once merrily play'd down the day,
    But where now only echoes the owl's eerie call.

There they whirl o'er the hearth where the fox has its
    lair,
In the stones tumbled down in the old ruin'd pile,
Where the baron once strode with a proud, dauntless
    air—
    The young maiden gliding in beauty the while.

And away where the village spire up thro' the trees
    Holds the holy cross high o'er the graves of the dead;
The ash and the beech sadly moan in the breeze,
    Their pride and their glory sere, wither'd, and red.

The leaves dolefully rustle the ridgy mounds o'er,
    When the moonbeams gleam in thro' the bare bend-
      ing boughs,
Where (the spirits all pass'd to eternity's shore)
    The weary frames rest in death's dreamless repose.

There the silver birch weeps, with its hair streaming
    long,
Which the winds of October tear off with a sigh;
As they wander the woodlands with sorrowful song,
    When the trees all are trembling and ready to die.

Yet oft the mild sunblinks smile down on the scene,
    When, calmly expectant, the earth seems to wait
For the wild storms of winter—the icy blasts keen
    Coming fiercely and fast through the far polar gate.

Now, timid and low, the lark sits on the lea,
  ' And the small birds flit silent far ben in the wood;
And though no storm is smiting the tumbling sea,
    Yet a hoarse boding sound comes afar o'er the flood.

And vainly we look for the white-bellied bird,
    Skimming swift thro' the air, at the close of the
        day;
For, soon as the first-falling leaflet is heard,
    Far, far o'er the sea, soars the swallow away.

Now, moaning afar, where the yellow woods wave,
    The winds come abroad with a sob and a sigh;

Like some spirit unshriven, at eeriesome grave,
　When the moon has gone down, with no star in the
　　sky.

So droop'd down the night with a dark troubled air,
　The rocking winds piping with shriek and with
　　pause,
When Martha, the moor-maid, sweet, gentle and fair,
　With fear undefined, from the fireside withdraws.

Long, long, she lay listening the loud roaring blast;
　When others slept sound, she felt awe-struck and
　　lone ;
Why shudder'd she so at the storm whistling past ?
　It oft she had braved at the grey rocking stone.

There to meet her own Edwin—that trysting place dear—
　She ofttimes would hie when the thunder roll'd loud,
With the hoarse tempest roaring, yet all without fear,
　She would wait for him there, 'neath the storm-
　　woven shroud.

He was true to her ever, and ever would prove,
　She could trust to him fully, though far from her then;

To heir a rich uncle, bring wealth to his love,

He had cross'd the wide sea, but would soon come
again.

His last loving letter had told her the day,

When the ship he would take for his own island
home;

His journey had prosper'd—the wide watery way

Would soon be recross'd, when no more he would
roam.

Thus she mused, yet her heart flutter'd fast in her
breast—

The good ship would soon bring him safe to that
shore—

Then why should that storm with such fears her molest,

When the shore here he'd reach not for two weeks
or more?

The midnight had pass'd ere sleep seal'd her sweet
eyes,

And it changed, but it calm'd not the grief of her
mind;

For in dreams she saw visions terrific arise,
  Which seem'd surging by on each blast of the wind.

Forms, wild with affright, waved their arms in the air,
  Then vanish'd from view with a heart-piercing yell;
Yet once more would appear, with a look of despair,
  While their sobbings of woe on her frighten'd ear
    fell.

Then she struggled for breath, for her life-blood it
    froze;
  She saw Death ope his arms, and Hope wave an
    adieu;
Just then, on the wind, a loud thunder peal rose—
  Her sleep then it broke, and the nightmare withdrew.

The climax had come with the storm, and a calm,
  With a lulling sigh, came with the dawn of the day;
And the robin's song soothed her pain'd ear like a
    psalm—
  The morning light chasing her fears fast away.

Oft thinking of Edwin, the hours glided on,
  And the red sun was sinking away in the west,

When a loving friend call'd at that cottage so lone,
  With a sorrowful face, and a heart ill at rest.

In tremulous tones he told how the ship,
  Which young Edwin had come in, had sail'd safe
    and fast;
And had reach'd, too, the shore (the words froze on his
    lip),
  But had struck on a rock—the wild waves' prey at
    last.

With a look full of anguish, a cry of despair,
  Martha rush'd from the house, held her brow to the
    breeze;
The daylight was fading—who striding on there
  Approach'd her so fast, through the wan birchen
    trees?

She knew that the ocean would yield up its dead,
  And all mankind come forth from the grasp of the
    tomb;
But not till the long destined ages had fled,
  And till quaked the wide world at the last trump
    of doom!

Confused, and amazed, she saw Edwin draw near;

His arms were around her, no spirit was he;

Half swoon'd she away, but of joy, not of fear,

To find him alive, whom she thought in the sea.

Few, few had escaped from a grave in the deep—

Clinging strong to the wreck, he was borne to the shore:

Other hearts long will ache, other eyes long will weep,

For lovers as true, they will see never more!

NOVEMBER.

NOVEMBER winds wail long and loud ;
    O'er hill and dale the dark storm-cloud
        Is like a curtain drawn ;
The trees sway with a dreary sigh,
As from the boughs the last leaves fly
        Along the cheerless lawn.
The streams, swoln by the teeming rain,
Down their rough channels foam amain,
Struggling as if in mortal pain,
        Through rocks which mar their course.
Great oaks are groaning in the wood,
Where but so late the ringdove coo'd,
And all the small birds sang and woo'd,
        Now swells the tempest hoarse.
The cold breath of the waning year
Fast makes the forest bare and drear,
        Though here and there is seen

A quivering ash, still fluttering fair,

With gaudy branches in the air,

    And leaves long, pendant, green.

Late does it feel the breath of spring,

But winter storms begin to ring,

Before its glory through the vale

Goes floating by upon the gale;

In summer heat or autumn chill;

In valley or on breezy hill;

Though winds sleep in the birchen brake,

And cause no curl upon the lake;

As if appall'd, it trembles sore

By day and night, for evermore,

Since of its wood the Cross was made

On which the Saviour bow'd His head.

    So eastern legends tell,

That when His life-blood oozed away,

And, awful, on th' affrighted day,

    A dreadful darkness fell,

Then on this tree, in every grove,

Though lightest breeze had ceased to rove,

    A strange, dread shudd'ring pass'd.

It trembles still, and ever will
(Though winds sink sleeping on the hill),
    Long as Time's ages last.

    In every glen, the trees, now bare,
Scream in the rough winds raving there,
But broad-coned fir-trees, fresh and fair,
    Give forth a dull deep moan.
Round alder bushes green, though thin,
Where brawls the brook its banks within,
And saddens with its sullen din
    The fields leaf-strewn and lone.
For now, no voice of blithesome bird
Through the far forest depths is heard ;
And where, so late, the rose bloom'd fair,
The wither'd, prickly briar is bare ;
And bare is now the hawthorn-tree—
In bloom the loveliest to see—
Still, here and there, o'er all the scene,
The tapering spruce is tall and green ;
And low down in the shelter'd glen
The laurel and the rhododen ;

And holly bright, with berries red
Around its gay, green prickly head;
And up the rent and riven wall
Of ruin'd Keep, where owlets call,
The ivy green still creeps and clings,
While robin by the blue burn sings,
As night winds wail, in mournful tune,
To ghostly shadows of the moon,
In eerie forms, thick glimmering through
The solemn branches of the yew.
In hedgerow, and in tangled scene,
Still twines the honeysuckle green;
The cherry-tree still shades the well,
And flutters yellow in the dell;
Though hoary winter, bleak and chill,
Sprinkles with snow the lone high hill.

To stubble fields, cheerless and bare,
The crows flock through the murky air,
    With hoarse discordant cry;
And where the sturdy ploughmen toil,
Guiding the ploughshares through the soil,

When the cold north winds sigh;
Croaking, they follow close behind,
And flutter in the wintry wind,
Till round the south has roll'd the sun,
His cheerless circuit early done,
While storm-blast gathers dim,
Struggles at first to feel its strength,
When, over sea and land at length,
Like giant great and grim,
It roars far through the groaning wood,
Rousing old Ocean's angry flood.
Or, when the pale sun's sickly ray
Hangs faintly on the skirts of day;
When winds sink down on moor and hill,
And cutting frost-breath binds the rill;
The big moon, sailing far on high,
Looks down with clear, cold, watery eye,
While shooting stars all round the sky
Rain down the steeps of heaven.
Paling the lesser light of star,
The streamers bright flash fast and far,
By viewless spirits driven.

All round the wide expanded arch,
Like God's great armies, see them march,
In red, blue, green, and white.
Though wheeling oft in strange array,
Yet noiseless is their rapid way,
Treading from off the fields of day,
On to the realms of night.
More dreadful shall these heav'ns appear,
When God to judge the earth draws near;
When stars shall through the ether rush,
And falling planets, planets crush;
When, wrapp'd together like a scroll,
The lurid heav'ns away shall roll;
When earth shall reel, and quake, and quiver,
And the great God-built mountains shiver;
When Ocean, with terrific roar,
Shall rush upon the sounding shore;
Who then with calm and tearless eye
Shall view Time's last great wave rush by,
And the heav'ns pass away?
Shall he whose wrath knew no restraints,
Who reel'd drunk with the blood of saints,

F

Through every ill-spent day;
Marching his squadrons to the field,
To butcher those who would not yield,
Like fierce Dalziel * at Rullion Green
(A Muscovite of savage mien),
Upon that dark November night,
When Scotland mourn'd the fatal fight
Of Pentland, bravely fought, though lost
By Covenanting battle host?
Though Paton's blows like lightning fell
On the fierce troopers of Dalziel;
And Captain Arnot's broad-sword swung
With giant force, on helmet rung;
And Auchens, too, a tow'r of strength,
Was borne by numbers down at length;

---

* When past sixty years of age, and when the affairs of Charles
II. had become desperate, General Thomas Dalziel, of Binns,
entered the Muscovite service under the Czar Alexis Michælo-
witch, who made him a general. He returned to Scotland in 1665,
commanded the Royal forces at Pentland in November 1666, and
kept imbruing his hands in the blood of the Covenanters till the
close of his life in 1685. Bishop Burnet says of him that "he
acted the Muscovite too grossly."

When, just as daylight waned away,
Blood and defeat closed in the day.
Then to the moors the saints were driven,
There slaughter'd, or to prison riven,
      For twenty years and more;
Still, would they not to tyrants yield,
But oft upon the scaffold seal'd
The truth, and dyed the wood and field,
      Undaunted with their gore.
Their graves are seen on hill and glen,
Dear, hallow'd spots to patriot men,
      Who keep the memories green
Of holy sires, and matrons too ;
And virgin martyrs, not a few,
Who pass'd death's gloomy portals through,
      With souls calm and serene.
And who shall calmest look at last,
When down the Judge's eye is cast
      On nations at His bar?
When kings shall no more wear a crown,
Nor captains touch their swords and frown,
      As when they march'd to war.

Then shall the feeble be the strong,

And through eternity prolong

    The note of victory's psalm.

No more to death, by earth's foes driven,

But happy now in smile of heav'n,

    They breathe its holy calm.

The Cross has ended in the Crown ;

Heaven's highest bliss for earth's brief frown.

DECEMBER.

DECEMBER sunbeams blink o'er field and fell,
   From the low chambers of the southern sky;
The bare trees stretch their shadows o'er the dell,
   Through which the brown brook foams and dashes
     by.

The dull cold sky leans low upon the hills,
   And clouds as cold creep down upon the land;
Strange boding sounds the whole wide welkin fills,
   And the sea waves surge eerie on the strand.

And where yon ruin'd castle crowns the height,
   The owl's wild scream at gloaming hour is heard;
As through the riven walls the moonbeams bright
   Show, flitting there, night's foul and lonely bird.

Red in the west has closed the eye of day,
   And, one by one, the twinkling stars appear;

While up the east the moon holds on her way,
   The lone and silent hours of night to cheer.

The winds have sunk, and bright and clear awhile,
   Flow floods of glory o'er the fields of heaven;
And starry train in radiant troops defile
   Upon those plains where angel hosts have striven.

The keen frost grasps the rivers and the brooks,
   Hushing their voices by its silent touch;
The broad lake like a burnish'd mirror looks—
   The angels bright may smooth their plumes at such.

The night glides on, the winds again awake;
   A grey film gathers over all the sky;
The storm-sprite moans on mountain and in brake,
   And o'er the desert moves with many a sigh.

The clouds grow dense, and, bursting forth amain,
   Whirls the white snow in dense and stifling mass;
The wild drift drives terrific o'er the plain,
   And, leagued with death, roars through the moun-
     tain pass.

With dawn of day how changed is all the scene!

The paths are block'd, the vales have disappear'd;

While, ever and anon, new hills between

Stand piled and peak'd, by snowy tempest rear'd.

Like sheeted ghosts appear the gloomy pines

High on the cliffs, and nod their heavy heads;

While round their stems the ivy twists and twines,

Keeping its hold, howe'er the tempest speds.

Clear in the frost the outline of the hills

Is vividly defined; beneath the foot

The frozen snow crisps coldly, and the rills

Give forth a strange sad sound, or else are mute.

Now is the time for Caledonia's game:

With broom, light heart, and keen, well-polish'd
stone,

The curler seeks the loch, ardent for fame,

Scorning the cold and cutting north wind's moan.

The farmer, laird, and labourer are there;

There lawyer, merchant, priest excited move;

Ply broom and stone, and with cries rend the air—
The hero he who best his skill can prove.

All else 'neath heaven's illimitable dome
  Is silent out among the snow-clad hills;
But loud the din when bloodless warriors come,
  And aim of conquest every bosom thrills.

Yet kindly feelings rise high in their hearts;
  And, ever mindful of the needy poor,
With ready will all act their generous parts
  To drive dread hunger from the poor man's door.

Now Christmas comes; no day of all the year
  Brought such glad tidings down from heaven to
    earth
(Our fears to banish, and our hopes to cheer),
  As when the angels sang the Saviour's birth.

The birds were mute in every bush and bow'r;
  But holy angels raised a sweeter song—
" Good-will and peace to men be from this hour;
  Glory to God in highest," sang the throng.

Far rang these heav'nly strains along the hills,
  And in among the overhanging rocks;
The holy sound, the long-drawn valley fills,
    Where, awed with fear, the shepherds fed their
    flocks.

Still rolls it down the corridors of Time,
  Inspiring hope in mortals here below;
Isles, continents, have caught the notes sublime,
  Which woo us back from the black gulf of woe.

Often, methinks, the lovely starry light
  Of heav'n beams softer on the Christmas morn;
Surely our hearts should grow more pure and bright,
  Since, unto all, the Sacred Babe was born.

Glad let our hearts be on this holy day,
  And pure through all our after course to come;
God of all goodness! let us no more stray,
  But guide and guard us to Thy blissful home.

How fast the years glide on and steal away!
  Like yesterday, this joyous time was here;

And now again returns the happy day,

  Though round since then has roll'd the circling
  year.

Soon the great ocean of the eternal past,

  Join'd to the eternal ocean yet to come,

Shall roll their dreadful waters, dark and vast

  O'er Time's small island, man's uncertain home.

Uncertain, for our days go gliding by,

  Swifter than ships wafted by mighty wind;

More rapid than the eagle in the sky,

  Faster than post, who dares not lag behind.

Like flow'r man comes, and like a flow'r he goes ;

  Like shadows flee his few short years away;

His days determined, soon his fix'd months close,

  When in the grave he mingles with the clay.

Where is the man who death shall never see,

  Or from the grave can rescue his own soul?

His threescore years and ten unnoticed flee ;

  Like tale that's told, the rapid cycles roll.

December! thou didst rob me of my sire;
  Chill blew Death's breath upon his dying bed;
With stealthy step he stole still nigh and nigher,
  While I held up a father's silver'd head.

For fourscore years and more he walk'd with God,
  And long had kept his journey's end in view;
And now at last he felt His staff and rod
  Support him in death's stream now passing through.

The end had come; but just before the close,
  From out what seem'd his last long sleep he woke;
His wasted hand from off his pale cheek rose,
  And with firm voice the silence thus he broke—

" God is our refuge and our strength, and He
  A very present help is; I'll not fear,
Though earth should be removed and mountains be
  Cast in the sea, while waves their foam crests rear.

Though mountains shake, and waters roar aloud;
  A river is whose sacred streams do glad

The holy place of the Most High's abode;

No sorrow there e'er makes His dear saints sad.

In midst of her the Lord our God doth dwell,

And nothing shall that city e'er remove;

Our God Himself shall help her, and right well

Shall keep all those who stand strong in His love."

He paused, and calmly pass'd through Jordan's wave;

A smile of triumph play'd upon his face;

Just as he pass'd, one last glad look he gave,

That look nought from my memory can efface.

'Tis long since then, and now my locks wax grey;

He first I saw enter death's gloomy vale,

But many since that dull December day

I've seen descend, 'mid many an anguish wail.

The road seems lonely, since we go alone

On our dark voyage to the unseen shore;

O! for the guidance of the Holy One,

To light the way, and quell the billowy roar!

Conclusion.

THE Circling Year completes its ceaseless round,.
   Time's silent wing has wafted it away;
How solemnly its parting footfalls sound
In the last hour of its dull cheerless day.
Softly they tread, but never once they stay,
As to the dim invisible they go;
Man, too, moves onward through life's battle-bray,
Leaves all his friends, 'scapes ev'ry treacherous foe,
Which, lurking, line the paths he needs must pass·
    below.

Yet pleasant spots adorn the way we take,
Deck'd with the early snowdrops of the year;
April's sweet primrose, beaming in the brake;
May's lovely lily, wet with dewdrop clear;
June's laughing rose, in hedgerow far and near;
The mountain pansy in the glowing light

Of July's rays ; and on the moors appear
The heather bells, when August suns shine bright
To which the honey bees, sweet murmuring, take their
   flight.

Journeying along, we see September's corn,
In golden shocks, gladden the fields afar;
The swallow brood awake the early morn,
Twitter and skim the air, till ev'ning star
Shines on the reapers; and the moon's pale car
Glows on the scene, silv'ring each tow'r and tree,
When storms sleep soundly, and nought comes to jar
The holy peace which reigns o'er land and sea,
Till sere October comes, and sets the wild winds free.

'Tis soothing e'en to hear November roar
In loud storm howling far among the hills;
To see fierce crested billows charge the shore,
And meteors glare upon dark dashing rills,
Whose fiery flash with awe the bosom fills.
'Tis bracing, too, to feel December's breath
Come from the north, when robin only trills

His ditty in the woods, while far beneath,
The frost-bound brook is held in the embrace of death.

Thus goes the year, and one again has gone
To swell the countless number of the past;
'Tis long since Time, in some mysterious zone,
Began its solemn march through cycles vast;
The coming gulf we gaze on, and aghast
Would fain go backward and retrace our course,
But fate forbids; our die's for ever cast!
Rills run not backward to their infant source;
And Time's strong stream flows on with never-failing
    force.

Each year that goes shortens the mazy stream;
Lessens the distance to the unseen land;
With ev'ry passing year, a nearer gleam
Of light comes beaming from heaven's emerald strand:
Where ransom'd saints and beck'ning angels stand
With palms of vict'ry in the bow'rs of bliss.
Guide us, O God! to join that glorious band;
Why should we stray, or slumber, and so miss
The joys that may be ours, lured to some dark abyss!

MISCELLANEOUS POEMS.

G

 MISCELLANEOUS POEMS.

PARAPHRASE OF HABAKKUK.

CHAP. III.

LORD, I have heard Thy speech and was afraid;
 O Lord, revive Thy work, thine own cause aid;
In mid-time of the years, O Lord, make known,
And ev'n in wrath, have mercy on Thine own.

God came from Teman, and the Holy One
From Paran travell'd in His strength alone.
His glory clothed the bending heav'ns around,
And wide o'er earth His praises did resound.
About His steps the thunderbolts burn'd bright,
And from His hand there glow'd great horns of light;
Yet hidden there was His Almighty power,'
While on before, His en'mies to devour,
The noisome pestilence stalk'd dim and dread,
Startling the living by the heaps of dead.

The earth to measure, rising from His seat,
Fierce flamed the burning coals around His feet.
The nations He beheld, and driv'n afar
Were all the people whose delight was war.
The eternal hills were scatter'd o'er the land,
And bow'd their heads beneath His lifted hand.
Strong is His arm, His everlasting ways
Are never hinder'd by His length of days.

On Cushan's quivering tents great anguish fell,
And where the curtains of the Midians swell,
Great trembling seized, and in the valleys low,
Where rivers run, was heard the wail of woe.
In consternation the sea-billows fled,
And moan'd far off from Thy strong war-steed's tread.
In fear, the streams forsook their wonted course,
And, troubled sore, rush'd backward to their source.
Lord, was Thy wrath against the rolling wave?
Or didst Thou smite the sea, Thine own to save?
That on Thy chariots of salvation Thou
Didst smite the wave, and through the ocean plough
A pathway for Thy people, and didst ride

Thy horses strong, their leader and their guide!
Thy bow was naked in Thy people's sight,
When Thou for them to battle didst alight.
The broad streams rolling swiftly to the sea,
Divided in the valleys were by Thee;
The mountains trembled, and the floods pass'd by,
Beneath the brightness of Thine awful eye.
Old Ocean's flood call'd from its deepest caves,
And flung on high its wild tumultuous waves;
Up in the heavens the flaming sun stood still,
The pale moon ling'ring on the western hill;
For, while Thine arrows flew on Israel's foes,
And sped Thy spear, the day refused to close.
Thy wrath did make the heathen nations mute,
Th' awed earth trembling underneath Thy foot.
For the salvation of Thy people Thou
Woundedst the head and scathed the haughty brow.
Thine arm, O Lord, did crush the heathen's might;
His sceptre fell before Thy presence bright.
The strong staves of thy tribes did strike them through,
When they to battle like a whirlwind flew;
Then, through the troubled sea's terrific roar,

Tumbling in wild commotion to the shore,

Thou walk'd Thy horses, where wild waves leap
   high,

And yawning gulfs like graves between them lie.

I heard the awful judgments, O my God!

Design'd for Israel by Thine anger's rod.

My belly trembled when the voice I heard;

My pale lips quiver'd, for I greatly fear'd.

Weakness and pain enter'd my rotting bones;

My troubled soul sent forth sad heavy moans

That I might rest, when Thy afflicting hand

Bring'st Chaldea's troops t' invade our stricken land.

Yet though no flow'r shall on the fig-tree blow,

Nor fruit of vine make the wine-fat o'erflow;

Yea, though the labour of the olive fail,

And barren fields bring the faint famine wail;

Though from the folds the fleecy flocks decay,

And from the stalls the herds decline away;

Yet in the Lord Most High will I rejoice—

The joy of God's salvation be my choice.

The Lord Jehovah is my strength, and He
Will make my feet like hinds' feet, fleet and free ;
And He, the conqueror, shall lead me still,
To sing His psalms, upon His holy hill.

———o———

LINES WRITTEN IN GLAISNOCK GLEN.

SWEET Glaisnock Glen,
    I love again,
When spring time is advancing,
    Through thee to stray,
    When day's last ray
Is on thy streamlets glancing.

    The thrush to hear
    Sing soft and clear,
To charm the dusky gloaming ;
    While nimble fly
    The grey bats by
Around me in my roaming.

On dewy wing,
Here soaring sing
The larks, when morn is blushing;
And round the lawn,
Where sports the fawn,
The blackbird's song is gushing.

The mellow cry
Of cuckoo shy
Deliciously is ringing;
While, rippling clear,
The burnie near
Its silver tune is singing.

Fair to the sight,
The primrose bright
In budding brake is gleaming—
Then comes the rose,
When summer glows,
With show'rs of sunshine streaming.

The soft green broom,
In golden bloom,
Then round the glen is glowing;

While o'er the linn,
With pleasant din,
The waters bright are flowing.

At every turn
The feathery fern
In fairy nook is flaunting,
While sweetest song
Gushes along
The glades, where birds are chanting.

In autumn day,
'Tis sweet to stray
Here, when the winds are sighing;
When saffron beams
And orange gleams
Down on the woods are lying.

When mountain bee
Hums drowsily,
Home through the tree-tops bending;
While lovers meet,
With kisses sweet,
In groves, when day is ending.

Here, coming fast,
Strange thoughts have pass'd
Across my mind in motion;
Of man's brief life,
With mysteries rife,
And of that vast, dim ocean,

To which we glide,
On Time's swift tide,
Our barks with base dross freighted;
Clear then the deck,
Lest wild shipwreck
Sees all our best hopes blighted.

Life's voyage past,
I reach at last
The blissful hills of heaven—
Methinks I'd sigh,
At times to fly
To this sweet glen at even,

And muse and stray
My wonted way,
When golden day is dying—

When its last light,
Melting in night,
Along the hills is lying.

Hear through the trees
The tuneful breeze,
Like angels sweetly singing;
Then glide once more
Back to that shore,
Where golden harps are ringing.

———o———

LINES ON AN EARLY SNOWDROP.

HAIL! first fair flow'ret of the year,
    The spring-time sweet foretelling:
Thou'rt beautiful, though winter's tear
    Still in thine eye is swelling.

The rough winds bend thy pale, pure head,
    When pass the storms careering;
When sinks the sun, all lurid red,
    Westward, as night is nearing.

Where brawls the burn beneath the brae,
    Its hidden path pursuing
Through lonesome, winding, woody way,
    Where the shy dove stands cooing

In fir-tree looming far on high,
    Through which the winds are wailing
Of winter, with its parting sigh,
    When by come storm-clouds sailing.

Here smil'st thou by the moss-grey stone,
    When sunny blinks are breaking
Through clouds high o'er the mountain's cone,
    Where larks hold merry-making.

Sweet flower! who tellest thou the time
    To come forth from thy sleeping;
When o'er thee, dead, through the year's prime,
    The summer dews are weeping?

The seal of death is on thee then,
    Though the warm sun, life-giving,
With leaf and flow'r decks wood and glen,
    Where sing the waters living.

The fair and fragrant lilies wave,
  And roses, too, are blooming
In spring and summer, round thy grave,
  The evening air perfuming.

So, where God's dear ones sleep in death—
  " Life's fitful fever " over—
There bloom hope's bays with balmy breath,
  And there the angels hover.

And He who brings each flower to bloom,
  Unerring in its season,
Shall wake the sleepers of the tomb,
  By power past human reason.

——o——

MONODY ON THE
DEATH OF WILLIAM WORDSWORTH.

Written in the Spring of 1851.

TIME, with light foot, thou travell'st on thy way ;
    And, over all, still hold'st thy potent sway ;
Man does thee homage with his hoary head,

When over him a few short years have fled ;

Feebly he totters down life's rugged road,

Then sleeps forgotten 'neath the grassy sod.

Thy touch, O Time ! destroys the mountain's side,

And blasts the oak in all its branchy pride ;

Low in the dust thou makest the city lie,

Whose lofty towers seem'd lasting as the sky.

The ocean roars, and, surging on the land,

Shatters the rocks, and licks away the sand ;

Slowly these waters of the mighty deep

Leave their old bed, and on the dry land creep.

Change steals o'er all, as thou, Time, glidest on,

Thy light foot marking even the marble stone.

Can nought, O Time ! resist thy steady force ?

Must dark oblivion follow still thy course ?

Must man for ever leave the earth, and go

To sleep forgotten in the dust below ?

Hail, genius, hail ! Thou light of Heaven appear,

Come from on high, the gloomy earth to cheer ;

Thy beams still blaze far back the track which Time

Has hurried over in his march sublime ;

Thy voice still rises from the shadowy sea

Of vanish'd years, which time has heap'd on thee;
Yes, thou canst nobly brave Time's furious shock,
And at the sweep of circling ages mock;
Canst strip oblivion of its sable crown,
And to the dust dash its dark sceptre down.

Come, then, O Muse, assist me while I sing
Of him whose genius on unwearied wing,
Soaring aloft, by native strength sustain'd,
Fame's ever-during temple now hath gain'd.

Wordsworth! O, if thy spirit leans to hear
This plaintive song, and mark the trickling tear,
Well dost thou know sincere the heavy moans,
The Muse now utters o'er thy mouldering bones.

Last of that band * whose genius blazed abroad,
Proving mankind the product of a God!
As o'er thy tomb the Muse now showers her tears,
Our thoughts in grief revert to bygone years,
Ere Time's swift river, sweeping still along,

---

* The great contemporary poets of the early part of the
present century.

Into the grave had swept those sons of song,
Whose strains celestial, wondering echoes caught;
Wide earth resounding with these gems of thought.

No more shall Crabbe of poor men's ills complain,
Nor Coleridge chant his all-unearthly strain.
No more shall Scott, far in some dusky dell,
Wake other strains like those we love so well.
Southey no more shall strike the world with awe,
Telling the wonders that *Kehama* saw.
Byron no more shall sing " The Isles of Greece ; "
And Shelley's burning brain is now at peace.
Dull death has stricken tuneless every tongue,
And all those bards their farewell songs have sung.

And thou, too, Wordsworth, following in the rear,
Hast pour'd thy last song on each listening ear :
No more shalt thou " revisit " Yarrow braes,
And add new beauty by thy living lays;
No more by lone St Mary's lake shalt stray,
And mark the swan " float double " on her way;
No more a wanderer o'er the mountains go,
To see the first and latest flow'rets blow;

Upon thine ear the babbling brook no more

That song shall pour it learn'd so long before,

Death's pale seal sits securely on those eyes,

That gazed enraptured on the starry skies,

And on thy noble, venerable brow

Death's wasting hand is working ruin now;

For unrelenting is that last stern foe,

And all must fall beneath his conquering blow:

Quick, though unseen, his secret darts are shed,

And spare not in their flight the honour'd head;

Into the gloomy grave the good are hurl'd,

And earth's best benefactors leave the world.

All at his bidding hurry hence away,

For death, dread monarch! brooks of no delay.

Now, o'er the land, Time's noiseless chariot sweeps,

The spring returns, the pure, pale snowdrop peeps

Through the cold earth, and smiles unto the day,

Which, lengthening, tells that winter hastes away.

Sweet Rydal!* soon thy storm-toss'd waves shall
    fall,

---

* A lake near Wordsworth's house.

H

And sink to silence at spring's joyous call ;
On all thy banks fair flow'rets shall appear,
And small birds sing to the advancing year.
But now thy Bard marks not thy wild flowers blow,
Nor hears his ear thy waters' tuneful flow ;
Where now that form, whose shadow oft was seen
At day's decline, along the lake serene,
As on thy banks at eventide he stood,
And watch'd the water lily, in the flood,
Close its pure bosom to the setting sun,
Withdraw its smiles, and sleep till night was down ?
The earth has claim'd its own—the soul's away,
The dust now mingles with its kindred clay ;
But if the just bend from Heaven's bright abode,
To mark those scenes their earthly steps have trode ;
If, from its radiant residence on high,
The soul e'er sweeps adown the starry sky ;
Then, on the balmy breath of fading day,
The soul through scenes it loved may often stray ;
There kiss the wild flowers on the lonely fell,
Stray by the stream that murmurs down the dell,
Far in the forest list the voice of song,

Then mount again to join the seraph throng—
There, by the streams of Paradise to stray,
And sing a new song through eternal day.

LINES ON AN OLD TREE.

OLD TREE, thy lengthy life is done,
   The woodman will not spare thee,
But plies the mattock and the spade
   About thy roots to bare thee.

The hand that planted thee has long
   Forgot its skill and cunning;
Its memory fading from the earth,
   As Time's sand-glass was running.

Thou wast a tall and stately tree
   Ere the steam horse, careering,
Devour'd the distance, or on sea
   The self-moved ships were steering.

Before Britannia's sceptre sway'd
  O'er India's swarthy nations;
Or the great empire of the west
  Had laid its firm foundations;

Before the lightnings of the sky
  Were tamed, and taught to bear
Man's messages o'er hills and seas,
  Thy boughs were spreading fair.

When in thy budding branches gleam'd
  The golden glints of morning,
How blithely there the wee birds sang,
  The coming winter scorning.

When corn-crakes call'd in clover green,
  And the cuckoo's plaintive lay
Fell soft on sighing lover's ear
  At the crimson close of day;

And when the new moon's silver rim
  Dipp'd to the western sea,
What pensive lovers hast thou seen
  Go musing o'er the lea!

Or lingering 'neath thy silver leaves,
   Stand fluttering, pleading, sighing,
With her who scarce would own the flame
   Of which the youth was dying.

When the fierce storm-sprite waved his wand,
   And wintry winds were wailing,
The raven oft to thy bare boughs
   Through the dark air came sailing.

There, on a bent and leafless branch,
   Would set him cawing, croaking,
While from the plain the hurricane
   Thy giant trunk was rocking.

And robin redbreast on a twig
   Would sit and sing so cheery,
Though icy gales came up the vales,
   All snow-clad, bleak, and dreary.

Oft didst thou see the men of old
   Trudging afoot to town,
Or seated on some sturdy cob,
   Come from the moorlands brown.

The father, with his lyart locks;
  The mother, silver grey;
The son, with lightsome lively air;
  The maid, like flow'r of May.

Time passing bring, on noiseless wing,
  Sad changes o'er them all;
The tottering limb, the eyeball dim,
  Presage Death's coming call.

The maiden's peachy cheeks wax pale,
  As seasons pass and go;
The flaxen locks wax few, the lips
  Lose life's young ruby glow.

Thou oft hast seen, as years swept by,
  Care furrowing every brow,
And mark'd the sigh heave the breast high,
  Where bright hopes wont to glow.

Thou, too, the merry marriage laugh
  Hast heard at evening hour,
Rise from light hearts which dreaded not
  Age or misfortune's power.

Ye baffled hopes and griefs but proved
    Life's constant, largest guerdon;
And thou that merry band hast seen
    Bending beneath life's burden.

And all in death slow borne away
    To that lone place of sorrow,
Where tears from many mourners' eyes
    Shall trickle till that morrow,

When monumental stones shall yield
    Their long-forgotten dead;
When Death shall die, and tears be dry,
    And vict'ry lift the head!

For in the happy, heavenly land,
    No ills the just are braving,
But palms of triumph every hand
    All joyously are waving.

Bright balmy June, with birds in tune,
    And buds and blossoms swelling,
Sees now no more, thee, old tree hoar,
    With silver leaves excelling.

Thy days are past; ours vanish fast,
They know no stop or staying;
Like streams that go, with ceaseless flow,
Still oceanward, though straying.

But why thus sigh for days gone by—
Days gone, and gone for ever!
Though 'gainst our will, Time bears us still
To dark oblivion's river?

We will not wail, we will not mourn,
Though life glides fast away,
But press on to that blissful bourne—
The land of endless day;

Where tall the leafy palm-tree grows,
Where winds life's crystal river;
Where the sun resplendent ever glows,
And gloomy night comes never.

——o——

P O M P E I I.

[Pompeii, with the neighbouring and sister City of Hercu-
laneum, was destroyed by a terrible eruption of Mount Vesuvius,
accompanied by an earthquake, in the year 79, during the reign
of Titus. So violent was the eruption, that some of the matter
thrown out of the crater was carried over to Africa, and some
accounts say even to the coasts of Syria. The cities were deeply
covered up with cinders, ashes, and stones, and not altogether by
lava, as was at first supposed. Marvellous as it may seem, great
streams of boiling water were also poured down from the burning
mountain upon the miserable inhabitants. About 145 years ago
much of Pompeii was disentombed, and many highly interesting
antiquities have since been discovered. Pliny, the naturalist, the
elder of that name, perished in the dreadful catastrophe.]

FAIR shone the sun upon Pompeii's towers,
    Green were her groves, and fragrant were her
       flowers,
Balmy the winds that o'er her gently blew,
Gladsome and bright the years that o'er her flew.
Happy her sons, blithe her fair daughters seem'd;
No heart foreboded ill, of evil no one dream'd.
In her gay course, although some prophet seer
Had solemnly proclaim'd her end was near,

The careless city would have laugh'd to scorn

The prophet sage, and hoped the coming morn.

But, ah! she little knew her end was near—

That next day's sun would close her gay career!

Day came, but darkness wrapt the land in night,

For sudden blackness gather'd on the sight;

Strange fitful gusts of wind came moaning by,

And swept Pompeii's streets with boding sigh;

Then, still as death, the breezes ceased to blow,

Back to their caves the whirlwinds seem'd to go;

Then, hoarse and deep, soon forth they rush'd again,

Roar'd o'er the land, and roused the sleeping main.

Above, Vesuvius Mount was heard to moan,

While the wide plain replied with many a groan:

Down to its deepest caverns shook the earth,

On whose affrighted face was hush'd the voice of mirth.

The temples trembled, and the idols shook,

And pale the priests to flight themselves betook;

To heaven imploringly they turn'd their eyes,

But as they look'd, high tow'ring to the skies,

Smoke and fierce flames from the high mountain went,

And with the thunder clouds soon closely blent;

Up to the darken'd heavens hot stones were hurl'd

(Where, dense and high, dark smoky columns
    curl'd),

Then, hissing madly, down the troubled air

They dash'd to earth, working dire havoc there;

While, far and wide, thick burning ashes flew,

Loaded the air, obstructed every view,

Blasted the arbours, scorch'd each towering pine,

And wither'd every mirth-inspiring vine.

More fatal far, and fast as northern snows,

Deep in the streets, the heaps of ashes rose,

Clogging the footsteps of the flying train,

Who fled for safety to the heaving main,

Where deep, and hoarse, and high, the billows
    broke,

As rose old Ocean at the earthquake's shock.

Pale, and appall'd, the trembling wretches stared,

As fierce and far volcanic lightnings glared,

Which, flashing through the thick sulphureous gloom,

Seem'd but to light them, living, to the tomb.

Loud cries of horror rose from every street,

And doleful groans, as cut off from retreat,

They sank exhausted near some falling pile,
And gasping, fought for life a little while;
Then stretch'd their limbs upon their burning bed,
And soon were number'd with the silent dead.

Loud roar'd the mountain, faster fell the shower
Of burning stones on garden, street, and tower;
Thick, and more thick, the scorching ashes fell,
Frequent and far was heard despair's wild yell;
For now, the angry hill sends hissing down
Streams of hot water on the fated town,
And stifling steam and poisonous vapours fill
All places now, and all things living kill;
Soon the mix'd deluge deeply covers all,
And death and silence on the fair town fall.
High o'er each tower, burnt stones and ashes lay,
And hid the city from the eye of day—
Hid it for long, but hid it not for aye.

Ages have pass'd, and cycles have gone by,
And once again Pompeii meets the eye
Of wondering mortals. Fair and fresh it seems,
But not again with busy life it teems;

Through every street a doleful silence reigns,
Sad and forsaken are her lingering fanes;
Death is the monarch here, for life has fled,
And claims not now this city of the dead!

———o———

LINES ON
THE DEATH OF A NEIGHBOUR'S DOG.

[Little "Tip" was an English terrier of almost matchless beauty. Her body was small, but it contained one of the largest and kindest of hearts. She could clearly reason, and draw inferences much more correctly than a vast number of the human race. She was a native of England, and was brought here far from her first home, and was accidentally killed at Cumnock, 9th August 1875, to the deep and abiding sorrow of her many attached friends.]

'TIS golden autumn's gladsome time,
    And round me flowers are blooming,
Yet, though the year is in its prime,
    Grief is my heart consuming

For thee, blithe "Tip," dear pretty dog,
    Whose bright, brief life is over,

For now thou tak'st thy last long sleep
    Under thy clay-cold cover.

Yestreen, in little cosy crib,
    Thou closed thy bright eyes gladly,
And dream'd, perhaps, of sports to-day,
    Which now have closed so sadly.

Or had'st thou no foreboding dream
    Of fleet-hoof'd steeds careering,
With death-like shadows round them thrown,
    As they thy home were nearing?

Thou answer'st not, by voice nor sign;
    But on came coursers prancing,
Who drove thy little body down,
    Beneath the bright wheels glancing.

A moment more! Thy collar bruised,
    Thy quick brain crush'd and broken!
What horror then seized thy wee heart,
    Shall ne'er by thee be spoken.

Anguish'd, I saw thy death-glazed eye,
    And thy love-telling tail

Grow still, and still for evermore,
  In Death's mysterious vale.

Men loved thee, and of kindred dogs,
  The crossest mongrel snarling
Ne'er laid an angry mouth on thee,
  Thou playful, docile darling.

I'll miss thy call at evening hour,
  I'll miss it in the morning;
I'll miss thy welcome as I pass,
  Toil travell'd, home returning.

Can that which thinks, can that which feels,
  As thou hast felt and thought,
Pass, perish from all space, away,
  And be a thing of nought?

Lie still, wee dog! lie still and sleep,
  All free from pain and sorrow;
Thou'lt maybe wake, and meet us yet
  On some far distant morrow!" *

---

* For thus giving expression to an opinion which I have long,
though not dogmatically, held to be highly probable, I shall no
doubt be laughed at by many, who, however, have never closely

When my own heart has ceased to throb,
And my last sun has faded,
Far down the dark ravine of death,
By earthly lights unaided,

May hearts as sad and full of love,
O'er my low grave be bending,
As mine was, when I saw dear "Tip"
Into her grave descending.

---

considered the subject ; and not a few, perhaps, will class me
with the "untutored Indian" mentioned by the poet Pope—

> "Who thinks, admitted to that equal sky,
> His faithful dog shall bear him company."

Many of the most philosophic minds in this and other
countries, have long held that at least the higher order of animals
have an immortality as well as man. St Paul also, the greatest
of all the apostles, in Romans viii. 19, and four succeeding verses,
to me, at least, very clearly declares the same thing. Paul, we
know, had a special revelation made to himself from God; and
for three full years after his miraculous conversion, he communed
with, and had visions and revelations from the Almighty, while
dwelling apart from the busy haunts of men, and amid the
sublime mountain solitudes of the Arabian peninsula of Sinai.
This view of that somewhat mysterious passage of Scripture
seems to me far more likely to be correct, than any of those
forced and arbitrary interpretations which I have generally seen
put upon it.

EXTRACTS FROM "THE INTERDICT."— AN UNPUBLISHED SATIRE.

EVENING SCENE NEAR EDINBURGH.

THE summer sun's last gorgeous gleam is gone,
  The breeze of night awakes with weary moan;
The fair full moon, half hid by sable clouds,
Now shows her face, and now her beauty shrouds.
Far in the south a single star displays,
Through breaking clouds, its soft and beauteous rays;
Edina's towers in gloom are almost lost,
And Leith, half hid, sleeps silent on the coast.
Dim in the darkness Arthur's Seat appears,
And a lone look Saint Anthon's Chapel wears:
Along the rugged hills strange echoes ring,
As round the rocks the night-winds sadly sing;
Borne on the blast, the knell of midnight hour
Falls on my ear from Saint Giles' ancient tower..

I

While thus I musing trode the neighbouring vale,

Strange murmurs pass'd me on the moaning gale;

Unearthly things seem'd sailing on the wind,

And forms all earthly follow'd fast behind:

Within Saint Anthon's gloomy walls they drew,

Where pale blue lights display'd the motley crew.

Terror awhile made all my bones to shake,

And horror grim my melting heart to quake;

But, calm at last, I raised my wondering eyes,

And turning thither saw strange sights arise.

On ebon throne there Satan's self was seen,

With deep-scarr'd visage, yet majestic mien;

Around his throne stalk'd many a giant form,

Subdued, yet wishing still heaven's towers to storm.

*   *   *   *

A THUNDERSTORM NEAR EDINBURGH.

SATAN arose, but sudden, ere he spoke,

Along heaven's arch the bellowing thunder broke;

Fierce lightnings flashing, fill'd the middle air,

The mountains seem'd to shudder at the glare

Which lighten'd every cliff and craggy steep,—

Trembling they totter'd to their centres deep.

Clouds roll'd on clouds, as flash it follow'd flash,

Thick fell the rain, while crash succeeded crash,

Gilt by heaven's fires, Edina's turrets shone,

In distant vales was seen each naked stone;

The ocean waves now beam'd like burnish'd gold,

Now in thick gloom the crested billows roll'd;

Now for a moment all was calm and still,

Then in an instant whirlwinds shook the hill.

*   *   .*   *

A MORNING SCENE NEAR EDINBURGH.

FAR o'er the ocean break the beams of day,

Gild the glad hills, and chase the night away;

Bright rosy rays upon the mountains gleam,

Glint through each grove, and glitter on each stream.

The gloom of night now flies before the morn,

And every murky cloud away is borne;

A balmy breeze is stealing o'er the earth,

Soft sunbeams call the wild-flowers into birth;

Above the mountain tops glad songs are heard,

Sung in sweet strains by morning's joyous bird.

The blithesome lamb is bleating in the vale,
And up the lone glen sounds the curlew's wail ; .
Along the shore glad voices greet the ear,
And gay boats bound across the billows clear :
The horrors of the night have pass'd away,
And peace and beauty come with coming day.

————o————

SUMMER EVENING.

NOW in the west the sun descends,
    'Mid blushing clouds his brow he bends
    Far o'er the ocean blue.
The beams he scatters as he flies,
Mount from the earth and gild the skies,
Though faint and fainter they arise,
    To meet the wanderer's view.
Fast from the east the night comes on,
Spreads her dark wing, and day is gone,
And every golden ray that shone
    On forest, lake, and hill.

The grove is silent: for no more
The thrush her notes melodious pour
From spreading oaks, whose branches hoar
    Wave o'er the gushing rill.
Soft zephyrs fan the wild-rose bowers,
And gently, on the closing flowers,
The silvery dew descends in showers
    Scarce felt, and all unseen.
The pale moon climbs the eastern sky,
As west away the sunbeams die;
Then shine the twinkling stars that lie
    Far in the blue serene.
The cuckoo's note * from yon green trees
Comes floating on the fragrant breeze;

---

* We have frequently seen it questioned, and once even by a
true poet of nature, whether or no the cuckoo continued its soft
monotonous cry through all the hours of night. We can assure
the reader that it does. The author's country occupation in early
life caused him to be out of bed for two whole nights very frequently, during the summer months ; and often has he delightedly
listened to its plaintive mellow voice all through the still hours
of the livelong night. The landrail's less pleasant cry is also
heard throughout the whole night, during the summer months, and
much more frequently even than by day.

The landrail's cry, the streamlet's tune,
The lake that sparkles 'neath the moon—
All blend their charms, and to the sight
And ear give exquisite delight.

———o———

LINES ON THE DEATH OF A WREN.

'TWAS evening, and the sunset glow
   Made streams in golden ripples flow,
Into the lakes which gleam'd below
   The calm, blue, bending heaven.
The flickering beams play'd on each height,
The birds, all round, sang with delight,
As hush'd and holy came the night
   On that fair summer even.

A thoughtless boy, I tripp'd along,
Singing some merry catch or song,
Wading the fair wild flowers among,
   Near to my father's cot.

A shining pebble in my hand
I carried from the stream's bright strand;
Oh! that my arm some wizard's wand
    Had palsied on that spot.

There, flitting on the cottage wall,
A little wren did hop and call,
And sweet its twee-twee-twee, let fall,
    All joyously and free.
Even yet my heart it deeply grieves,
And sharpest pangs my soul receives;
For still I see it on the eaves,
    Eyeing, but trusting me.

A murdering tom-cat, cruel, sly,
Crept round an angling wall close by,
It made to spring, and then did I,
    To save the singer sweet,
Straight at the cat the pebble throw;
In fear the bird flew up, when, oh!
The cat was miss'd, the wren struck low—
    It fell dead at my feet.

Warm in my hand, with tears and cries,

I took it up, I oped its eyes,

But dim were they, nor groans nor sighs

    Could pierce its death-closed ear.

In agony, I tore my vest

Wide open, held it to my breast;

Its little heart, still and at rest,

    Now felt no pain nor fear.

The mellow light of summer day

Was dying on the hill-tops grey,

When, lined with moss, in the cold clay

    I made its little grave.

The weeping birch bedew'd its bed,

And there as burning tears I shed,

As e'er were shower'd upon those dead,

    No love nor pray'rs could save.

By the same Author,

POEMS, LECTURES, AND MISCELLANIES,

Price 3/.

—o—.

OPINIONS OF THE PRESS.

. Dr John Francis Waller, late Editor of "The Dublin University Magazine," says,—" I recognise you as a brother, both in prose and verse. To have attained to such a literary position as you have, gives proof of true genius, which ever rises, no matter under what adverse circumstances."

The Rev. C. H. Spurgeon says,—"Mr Todd writes in a capital style, and with much poetic feeling."

The late Rev. Geo. Gilfillan says,—"Mr Todd's poems are characterised by a pervading enthusiasm, and by a general correctness and energy of expression. He goes to all his literary work with right good spirit, thorough sincerity of purpose, no small discrimination of judgment, and so *valeat quantum valere potest.*"

"The Scotsman" says,—"Mr Todd's inspiration is never fictitious; he writes as he thinks and feels, and as his thoughts and feelings are controlled by educated taste, all he has written will well repay perusal."

"The Ayr Advertiser" says,—"Lest we may be thought partial to an Ayrshire author, we, in justice to him, endorse 'The Scotsman's' criticism."

"The Ayr Observer" says,—"In Mr Todd's poetry there is much vivid description and smooth versification. His description of a thunderstorm reminds us of the majestic sweep of a Dryden and the polish of Pope."

"The Montrose Standard" says,—"We have read all the productions in Mr Todd's volume with unflagging interest, and closed the volume with a wish that there had been as many more yet to come."